The promise i
shiver with f
want to acknowleage or give in to.
"Forget it. I'm not interested in
a one-night stand, and that's all
you're offering, isn't it, Win?"

His fingers curled around her upper arm. "I made my feelings on marriage plain the day I interviewed you, but there's a whole lot of ground between a one-night stand and marriage. I never said I wasn't interested in any kind of commitment. I can guarantee you that while you share my bed, no one else will." His eyes narrowed. "You aren't going to convince me that you've married every man you've slept with."

The warmth of desire she had been feeling shifted to a frozen sort of pain. Win was like all the others, making assumptions based on how she looked and not *who* she was.

Lucy Monroe started reading at age four. After going through the children's books at home, she was caught by her mother reading adult novels pilfered from the higher shelves on the bookcase... Alas, it was nine years before she got her hands on a Mills & Boon® romance her older sister had brought home. She loves to create the strong alpha males and independent women who people Mills & Boon® books. When she's not immersed in a romance novel (whether reading or writing it), she enjoys travel with her family, having tea with the neighbours, gardening, and visits from her numerous nieces and nephews. Lucy loves to hear from readers. E-mail her at LucyMonroe@LucyMonroe.com, or visit her website: www.LucyMonroe.com

Recent books by the same author:

THE RANCHER'S RULES (Modern Extra)
TAKEN: THE SPANIARD'S VIRGIN (Modern™)

WHAT THE RANCHER WANTS...

BY
LUCY MONROE

MILLS & BOON
Pure reading pleasure

First published in Great Britain 2007
Harlequin Mills & Boon Limited,
Eton House, 18-24 Paradise Road, Richmond, Surrey TW9 1SR

© Lucy Monroe 2007

ISBN 978 0 263 85398 8

Set in Times Roman 10½ on 12½ pt
171-1007-47492

Printed and bound in Spain
by Litografia Rosés, S.A., Barcelona

Dear Reader

When I was writing THE RANCHER'S RULES—which was published in Modern Extra in November last year—a secondary character, Carlene Daniels, grabbed onto my heart and wouldn't let go. As she faced Grant's rejection with such wistful sadness, I knew I had to write her story. But who could she fall in love with?

Well, Win Garrison is even more stubborn and alpha male than Grant, and a heck of a rancher too. The only problem is his deeply seated aversion to marriage. And, despite how it may seem, Carlene wants nothing less. These two characters challenged me to write a story worthy of them, and I truly hope I have.

Enjoy!

Lucy

For my children...your support means the world,
and no mom could be prouder of what amazing
women and young man you have become

CHAPTER ONE

CARLENE DANIELS parked her car in the circular drive in front of the most imposing ranch house she'd ever seen.

Being from oil-rich Texas, she'd seen a few too…not to mention the beautiful homes built locally by millionaire celebs looking for *anonymous* vacation homes.

Anonymous. Right.

Built in the California Mission style, this home's three-story stucco walls gleamed pristinely in the bright sunshine, the red-tiled roof and wrought-iron accents looking elegant rather than historic. She wondered who lived here. Typical for the area, the ad had given no particulars about the family she would be working for. *If* she would be working for them.

Sunshine Springs was not a hotbed for career opportunities, especially for an ex-schoolteacher turned cocktail waitress. But it was time to stop hiding behind spandex miniskirts and her job at the bar. Her experiences with Grant Strickland had made her realize that.

She'd left Texas in pain and determined to leave her old life behind completely. When the only opening available when she arrived in town had been working in a bar, she'd taken it because in no way would it remind her of the job and the kids she'd loved so much back home. But memories didn't go away with a change in setting and she wanted her life back.

Carlene opened her car windows a crack and put a sunshade on the dash to protect the car from turning into a portable oven before sliding out of the driver's seat and slamming the door. Swinging the wrought-iron gate open to the entryway, she slipped inside and rang the doorbell. After a couple of minutes and no answer, she rang it again.

They were advertising for a housekeeper after all. If the bell hadn't been answered by now, it probably hadn't been heard.

The door swept open. "What's the rush?"

The husky, masculine demand caught her completely off guard. Oh, wow…this man was…totally yummy. Black hair, cobalt-blue eyes and a tall, drool-worthy muscular body.

"I…uh…"

The piercing blue gaze traveled from her hair to her toes and back up again. Then it made a return journey, leaving chills in its wake. Wow…again.

She knew what she wanted him to see: a woman

from another time in her life, before she'd taken the
job as bartender at the Dry Gulch. A time when her
clothes and manners matched the woman she was on
the inside.

Instead of the revealing outfits she wore to work
nowadays, she had donned a long straight denim
skirt, a loose white scooped-neck top, and white
sandals. Flats. After months of wearing nothing but
spiked heels that added inches to her diminutive
height, these shoes almost felt as if she were wearing
bedroom slippers.

The only concession she'd made to the glitz
she'd grown accustomed to was the silver and tur-
quoise belt around her hips. Even her normally
riotous brown curls had been tamed in a loose
French braid and she'd left off everything but the
barest of makeup. She looked exactly like what she
wanted to convey: a nice girl. Non-threatening in
the feminine stakes and perfect for the role of
housekeeper.

She stifled a cynical snort at the thought. Even her
oversized top could not disguise her generous
curves. Curves that had been causing her trouble
since the sixth grade. And she was pretty sure it was
those curves that had caused the second once over
and small tilt at the corner of the man's otherwise
rather grim lips.

However, she was darned if she was going to have
breast reduction surgery, as her mother had suggested

in order to make herself appear more respectable. She liked her figure. She just didn't like the things it made people assume about her character. An old familiar ache tried to work its way to the surface and she forced it back down.

That part of her life was over. She wasn't going to let it dictate her present any longer and she sure as shootin' wasn't going to let it dictate her future.

"You Carlene Daniels?"

She nodded, experiencing an odd inability to speak.

"I'm Win Garrison. Expected someone older."

"So did I." The words were out before she even realized she was going to say them.

She'd set this interview up with the former housekeeper. The woman had spoken little English, adding no further details about the family she was leaving behind than the ad had given. All Carlene knew was that Rosa's last day had been yesterday and that she, Carlene, had an interview for the position of housekeeper with Rosa's former employers today.

However, Carlene had heard of Win's ranch, the Bar G. Who hadn't? Only it had never occurred to her that the owner of a ranch that bred free-range mustangs, not to mention having the most prestigious thoroughbred horse breeding and training program this side of the Rockies, would be younger than fifty. Win Garrison was maybe thirty, but certainly not much older.

Making no effort to respond to her comment, he turned around and started walking down the hall, clearly expecting her to follow him. "I'll interview you out in the courtyard."

She walked behind him, cataloging his attributes like an inventory control clerk and powerless to focus her attention elsewhere. Despite his obvious wealth, Win's clothes were that of a working cowboy. His long legs were encased in a pair of jeans washed to a comfortable, faded softness that clung to his backside with almost indecent snugness. His ebony hair brushed the collar of the dark T-shirt that rippled with his muscles as he walked.

The man was too hot for Carlene's peace of mind. Maybe this job was not such a good idea…but hand-tooled boots clicked on the tile floor ahead of her drawing her inescapably toward a future as uncertain as the past she'd left behind.

Where was his wife? Why would *he* conduct the interview for a housekeeper and cook?

Win led her through the entrance hall to another interior hallway that surrounded the courtyard. An intelligent concession to central Oregon's cold winters, she thought. They went outside through one set of four sliding glass doors placed in the walls of windows that faced the courtyard from the house. She followed him to a large brick patio and couldn't help but admire the beautifully kept foliage along the way. Small shrubs and patches of grass, broken by stone pathways leading to the house, surrounded a two-tiered cement fountain. "It's lovely."

"Thank you."

He moved forward and pulled out a chair from the wrought-iron patio set. She sat down.

"Want anything to drink?"

She shook her head. "I'm fine, thanks."

He nodded and sat across from her.

When he didn't immediately begin asking questions, she decided to ask a few of her own. "Mr Garrison, I'm afraid I have almost no information regarding you and your family. When I called on the ad in the paper and spoke to your housekeeper, she told me little more than that she planned to be gone as of yesterday. Do you have children? Will Mrs Garrison wish to interview me as well?"

It made her nervous to have to go through a two-interview process for the job of housekeeper, but she would survive. It just meant that much longer before she knew whether or not she had the position. What she really wanted to ask was if there had been a lot of other applicants.

He leaned back in his chair, his boots scraping on the stone tile. "No."

No? No, what? She smiled faintly. "Would you care to expand on that a little?"

"No kids. No wife. No other interview."

She wasn't sure if she was relieved or worried by

that bit of news. "Then perhaps you would like to commence with this one?"

His eyes narrowed. "You sure you wouldn't like to do it? You seem to be doing fine so far."

Crud. It was the teacher's instincts coming out again. She would have thought, after all this time out of the classroom, she'd have no problem treating adults differently than the children she used to work with. But then a lot of times patrons at the bar needed the same kind of handling.

She tried another smile. "Um…okay. We can get the rest of my questions out of the way first. Is this a live-in position?"

"No."

She managed to bite back a sigh of relief. The job of live-in housekeeper to a man as good-looking as the one before her was rife with the potential for gossip. The last thing she wanted was any more gossip. "What are the hours, then?"

"Rosa worked from seven-thirty to four."

Carlene nodded. "What exactly do the duties entail?"

He frowned and shrugged.

She stared at him in shock. "You don't know?"

"Why do you think I need a housekeeper? It's the house stuff. I don't want to have to worry about it. A cleaning service comes in a few times a week. Rosa took care of setting that up."

Great. His Spanish-speaking housekeeper had set

up the cleaning service…which meant that the maids probably spoke Spanish as well. She could hope they were bilingual because her college French wasn't going to do her a lot of good here.

"What else did Rosa do?"

Win's frown deepened. "I told you…I'm not sure. I run my ranch and the stables. She ran the house."

"And that's what you want me to do…run the house?"

He nodded, almost smiling. "Yes."

"Did Rosa cook all your meals?"

"Yes. Both for me and the hands."

"Okay." Now they were getting somewhere.

"Did she make your bed?" Oh, nuts…why had she asked that? Not that she didn't need to know, but she really didn't need to be thinking about bed and this man in the same sentence.

But Win looked as if he was thinking. "The service only comes in maybe three times a week… my bed is made every night when I climb into it, the towels and such are gone from the bathroom too. Yes…guess she made my bed."

"And did the laundry." Not to mention a pile of domestic stuff that Carlene was quickly coming to realize Win never even *thought* about.

Must be nice to be rich enough to leave all those details to someone else.

"Well, yeah."

"It sounds like you want to hire a wife," she quipped.

He didn't smile at her small joke. Instead, his brows drew together in his fiercest frown yet. "The last thing I want is a wife, hired or otherwise. If you've got any ideas in that direction, we might as well part company right now."

She experienced an odd combination of amusement and anger at his words. Amusement that anyone could be this blunt and anger that he would assume she was angling for such a thing.

Okay, so she *had* come to the conclusion that she wanted the husband, the white picket fence and the two point five children playing in the yard after the last decent guy she dated ended up married to someone else. And she wanted that yard well manicured, not full of rusty automobile parts. The guys she met at the Gulch had not been candidates for the "two point five kids and white picket fence" scenario. They were generally interested in one thing and, with her figure, they expected to get it.

But there was no way that Win Garrison could know about her secret dreams and she certainly hadn't implied she was auditioning him for the role of husband in them.

"I'm here to apply for the position of housekeeper, not wife. Furthermore, I'm certainly not interested in marriage to a man who thinks monosyllabic replies pass for communication and rudeness is socially acceptable behavior. Don't worry. If I were to take the job of your housekeeper, your unmarried status would remain perfectly safe."

"Good." He looked satisfied, her insults seeming to go right over his head. "Then we can finish the interview."

She stood up. "I don't think that's a good idea, Mr Garrison." That she was using his rudeness as an excuse to get away from a man she was far too attracted to was not a thought she wanted to contemplate at the moment. "Thank you for your time, but I think it's best if I leave."

There had to be another job she could get that would get her out of the Dry Gulch and maybe make her application to teach in the Sunshine Springs school district a little more appealing. Just because this was the first good prospect she'd seen in the two weeks since she started looking, didn't mean it was the only possibility.

"Sit down, Carlene, and call me Win."

"No, really. I need to go." She turned to leave.

But his voice stopped her. "I said sit down." His tone made the quietly spoken command more intense than shouting could have.

She turned back to face him.

He smiled and her stomach dipped and that was so not good. "If you can't follow one simple direction, we're going to have a pretty rough working relationship."

Frowning, she remained standing. "I don't think we can have a working relationship at all, Mr Garrison."

"Why? Because I sometimes talk in monosyllable?"

"No. Because you *are* rude and I don't work well with rude people." It was the truth. She'd gotten chewed out more than once at the Dry Gulch for taking a bad-mannered customer to task for their behavior.

"If I apologize, will you finish the interview?"

She didn't think he was the kind of man that apologized often. "It depends."

"On what?"

"On why you were discourteous to begin with."

"What exactly did you consider the discourtesy, if you don't mind me asking? My one-word replies or my warning?"

She felt herself blush because she'd been rude too. Insulting even and it hadn't gone over his head. He'd simply opted not to make an issue of it.

She sighed. "The warning. Most women would not find your assumption that they are looking at you as a potential mate on such short acquaintance flattering."

Even as she said the words, she felt silly. She was taking them far too personally. Really.

His cynical laugh didn't make her feel any better. "Honey, I'm a rich man with a lifestyle a lot of people covet. A fair number of women would consider marriage a nice way to ensure they share it. I learned a long time ago to make my lack of interest in marriage clear from the beginning, no matter what relationship between me and the woman." He certainly wasn't talking in single syllables right now.

"You mean you warn all your dates and hands the same way?"

"Yes. I don't have any women working the Bar G right now, but the female vet got her warning the first time she came out to check the horses."

"It's like a religion with you," she said, a little awed by his vehemence.

He sat up, planting his booted feet securely under him. "You could see it that way. You sure talk fancy for a housekeeper."

But not for a high school English teacher with a degree in French literature, she thought. "Is that a strike against me?"

"I don't know. Why don't you sit down and we'll discuss it?"

She acquiesced.

He smiled again and she decided that she preferred it when he frowned. His smile was entirely too sexy and the last thing she needed was to think of her employer, particularly this one, as sexy in any way. He wasn't interested in marriage and she wasn't interested in an affair.

That left *sexy* out of their equation.

"What kind of experience do you have?" he asked.

"Not a lot," she admitted. "Not any paid, but I can cook and I've been keeping house for myself since I went away to college."

Of course, keeping up with her dorm room and then small apartments was nothing on the scale of his three-story mansion, but she would cope.

"If you can cook as well as you talk, the hands are going to love you." He gave her another once-over, this time, instead of chills, his gaze making her go hot in places an employer should not affect. "Then again, once they get a look at you, they'll think they've gone to heaven even if your food tastes like cow pies."

This she was used to. This she could handle. At least that was what she tried to convince herself. Men had been making comments about her figure for years. She had learned long ago that the best way to deal with the comments was to ignore them. "Ever eaten any?"

"Any what?"

"Cow pies?"

"No," he said, with a hint of smile in his voice.

"Then I guess you won't know if my cooking falls under that category, now, will you?"

The smile became a full-blown chuckle. "Guess not. You start tomorrow morning, Tex."

"My name is Carlene."

"But you talk like a Texan."

"I'll have to work harder on that. I'll never live there again." Too much pain she never wanted to revisit.

Relaxing against the brown leather couch in his living room, Win swirled the whiskey in his glass before taking a swallow. It had been several hours since Carlene Daniels had left. His new housekeeper. He grinned.

She had a body that would make most men uncomfortable in their jeans and talked like a prissy little schoolmarm. Remembering the curves her loose top had been unable to hide, he amended his thoughts. The lady wasn't exactly little, at least not in some places. She wasn't too big either. She was a perfect pocket Venus, with womanly curves that led to a naturally small waist. She was the stuff of most adolescent male dreams, maybe most adult ones as well.

She'd certainly been the subject of too many of his waking thoughts today. He still couldn't figure out what gremlin had gotten into him and prompted him to offer her the job. She had no experience. He sure as hell hoped she could cook. His hands might like looking at a sexy woman like her, but that would grow old pretty darn quick if she didn't feed them right. He sighed.

Maybe he should assign Shorty to help her until she got used to the routine. The diminutive man made lousy biscuits, but he knew the quantities and types of food horsemen ate.

She'd probably talk Shorty's ears off. The woman had a mouth on her and it was plain as the day was long that she was used to being in charge. So long as she limited that bossy streak to the house, they wouldn't have any problems. He didn't want to have to worry about anything but running the Bar G and Garrison Stables. With mares ready to foal he didn't have time to concern himself with stuff like meals and cleaning house.

He wondered where she'd gotten such a bossy streak. If she didn't have any experience as a house-keeper and cook, what types of jobs had she held before? He couldn't believe he hadn't asked her. He hadn't even asked her to fill out an employment application. He had hired her based on sheer instinct and that wasn't like him. He was a careful man.

He hated admitting it, but his hormones had played their part too. It was disconcerting to realize that he'd reached the age of thirty and he could still be swayed so strongly by the sight of a beautiful woman. He'd just gone too long without. He hadn't had a date in months and hadn't slept with a woman in even longer. He'd gotten tired of the games. Tired of empty sex. Both things seemed to come along with the territory for a man uninterested in marriage.

There were times the big house felt empty too, times he felt empty. His certainty that marriage was for idiots didn't waver. He'd learned the lesson too well at his mother's knee. Hadn't she married five men and divorced four? The only reason she hadn't divorced her last husband was because she'd died before she could get bored again with marital bliss.

There had been a time when Win had been willing to believe that there were women out there that weren't like his mother. He'd been young and foolish. Barely out of high school and overwhelmed with the responsibility of caring for his thirteen-year-old sister, he'd met a shy, sweet little gal who wanted to get married—Rachel. He had believed that Rachel could help with his sister, could make their household, devastated by the death of his mom and stepdad, a home again.

It hadn't worked that way. Rachel had wanted him to sell the Bar G and move to the big city. She had dreams and no one was going to stand in her way, least of all her young husband and his needy little sister. He hadn't wanted to risk marriage since then. He'd learned his lesson the hard way, but he *had* learned it.

Carlene sure had been offended when he laid it out flat for her. She'd bristled with feminine pride and it had been all he could do not to laugh. She was naïve if she thought most of the women who entered his life didn't see him as a potential meal ticket complete with caviar and silver spoons.

She didn't know it, but it hadn't been rude for him to set things straight from the beginning. It had been fair and he was a fair man. She had a right to know where he was coming from. He wanted her and he meant to have her, but he wasn't interested in marriage.

He'd wanted her from the moment he opened his door, irritated by the second ringing of chimes set off by the impatient person waiting on the other side. The woman standing on the other side had been so far from what he'd expected that he'd felt sucker punched. And horny.

No doubt about it. He had been too long without the company of a woman, but he'd had the good sense to hire Carlene and soon that would be rectified.

CHAPTER TWO

CARLENE liked Shorty, the ranch hand Win had assigned to help her in the kitchen, the minute she met him. He had a grin that more than made up for his lack in stature. Soft gray eyes twinkled under a crown of silvered hair. "Well, missy, Win says you don't got a hill of beans in experience, but I'm to help you learn the ropes. You know anything about cooking?"

She laughed. "I'd have to be pretty dumb to take a job as housekeeper and cook if I didn't, now, wouldn't I? Do I look dumb to you?"

Shorty sized her up as if he was seriously contemplating his answer to that question and Carlene's respect for him went up a notch. The man kept his eyes focused mainly on her face.

"No, missy, you don't look dumb at all. That must mean you can cook." He sighed with relief. "It's a good thing. Win and the hands ain't real fond of my vittles."

Then why had Win assigned the man to help her in the kitchen? Shorty answered that question for her with his next statement. "None of the hands, including our boss, can do any better. At least I know how to cook food without burning it, even if it isn't real appetizin'."

Carlene walked over to the sink and washed her hands. "I'll let you in on a little secret, Shorty. I can cook without burning the food and I've been told that my food is better than passable by more than one person."

"Well, glory be, that's a relief."

Carlene hoped that the rest of the ranch hands would share Shorty's enthusiasm when they filed into the large kitchen for lunch. She'd made French dip sandwiches, Caesar salad and cookies for dessert.

Win took a seat at one end of the table. Shorty sat to his left and a man they called Joe, who looked about the same age as Win, sat to Win's right. He was introduced as the ranch foreman in charge of the horse and mustang training. Four other hands, ranging in age from just out of high school to another man who looked as wizened and gray as Shorty, sat down. Apparently, most of the hands worked for Joe, while Shorty and one of the youngest men, a brunette with cold gray eyes they introduced as Lonny, worked in the thoroughbred stables with Win.

Carlene placed filled plates in front of each man, beginning with Win. She didn't realize that she'd been waiting for his approval until he looked up and nodded. "Looks good."

She quietly said, "Thank you," and continued passing out plates, feeling ridiculously pleased. After serving everyone, she turned back to the counter where she had lined up the ingredients for the pies she planned to make.

"Aren't you going to eat with us, ma'am?" Joe asked.

She turned around, waiting to see if Win would second the hand's invitation to join them. When he didn't, she replied, "I'll eat later. I've got work to do."

"Aw shucks, ma'am, we'd be pleased for your company," a redhead said.

Lonny gave Carlene a knowing look and patted the bench next to him. "You can sit right here, Carlene."

Normally, she would have just laughed off an invitation like that from such a young man, but there was an intensity about Lonny that made Carlene nervous. The cold ruthlessness in his eyes reminded her of the student that had torn her life in Texas to shreds. She suppressed a shiver, reminding herself that there was no disgruntled principal here to help Lonny hurt her. There was just Win and she could not see him stooping to the lengths her ex-boss had even if she rejected him.

She managed to swallow a rude comeback to

Lonny's comment, not wanting to offend Win's other employees her first day on the job. "No, thank you. As I said, I've got work to do."

She shifted her gaze to Win, wondering what he thought of the exchange.

The look he was giving the younger man was cold and deadly. He turned slightly so that he was looking directly at her, his gaze warming several degrees. "Do what's comfortable for your schedule, but don't skip your lunch."

She smiled at the order. "Yes, boss."

He nodded. "If you're hungry now, the men'll move so you can sit by Shorty."

It didn't escape her notice, or that of his men, if Lonny's narrowed eyes were an indication, that Win's dictate would place her next to him as well. Carlene didn't mind. Compared to Lonny, Win was a much safer bet. She had no doubt that sitting between him and Shorty she wouldn't have to fend off any roaming hands under the table.

She considered Win's offer. It shouldn't be such a big deal, but it would set a precedent for the future. If she ate with them now, human nature dictated that the hands would recognize that whenever she shared their table, her place would be between Win and Shorty.

Her stomach chose that moment to make a rumbling sound and the men laughed while she smiled, embarrassed. "I guess I'll eat now."

* * *

Several hours later after preparing a dinner that only required Shorty to heat things through before serving them, Carlene got ready to leave. Her feet didn't hurt as much as after a night tending bar, but her back ached from a different kind of labor. She'd spent the day cooking, cleaning and trying to decipher the written instructions Rosa had left behind in a confusing mixture of Spanish and English.

She wondered what had caused the other woman to abandon her job so abruptly.

"You sure know your way around a ranch kitchen," Shorty commented from behind as she pulled off her apron and hung it on the hook by the refrigerator.

She turned and smiled at him. "Thanks. I grew up in west Texas cow country."

"Congratulations, Shorty. You got more information out of her in five minutes than I was able to do during her interview."

Carlene's head snapped up at the sound of Win's amused voice from the doorway to the dining room. He leaned against the doorjamb, a lazy smile on his face and looking handsome as sin. He was dressed much as he'd been for her interview, except today his T-shirt was black instead of dark blue and a cowboy hat hung loosely from his fingers next to his thigh.

She wished he'd stop smiling at her like that. It made her forget what she was going to do next.

Forcing herself to focus on his words and not his mouth, she said, "You didn't ask."

He came into the kitchen sniffing at the casserole in the oven with an appreciative air. "Smells good."

"Thank you."

He lifted the linen towel covering the two marionberry pies she'd made for dinner. She'd used the native Oregon fruit, figuring the men would appreciate the plump, tangy blackberry-style filling. "You're wrong, you know," he said as he put the cover back over the pies.

"Wrong about what?" she asked, feeling breathless for no apparent reason.

"I did ask." He turned to face her. "I distinctly remember asking if you had any experience."

"You asked about experience as a housekeeper and cook. I don't have any formal experience, but I do know how to cook and clean house. I told you that."

She didn't understand his enigmatic expression. He asked, "Why'd you leave Texas? Were you looking for adventure?"

She couldn't hold back the laughter that bubbled forth. "If I'd been looking for adventure, I wouldn't have ended up in Sunshine Springs." Though the small town was a lot more than what she'd thought it was when she'd first arrived.

She'd had no idea at the time that it was a winter playground for the rich and famous.

He relaxed his tense posture and returned her smile. "No. You wouldn't have."

"So, why did you leave?" Shorty asked, reminding Carlene of his presence.

"It was time to move on," she replied noncommittally.

"Leave behind a disgruntled lover?" asked the irrepressible Shorty.

Carlene frowned. It was too near the truth. "I left behind a life that didn't fit me any longer."

Win's expression turned distinctly chilled. "Did that life include a husband? Children?"

"No." She was inexplicably hurt that he would have such a low opinion of her as to believe she would leave her own children behind, and her voice came out tight. "I've never been married."

His expression didn't lighten. "Do you do that often?"

"What? Move on?" Was he worried that she would move and leave him in the lurch looking for a housekeeper as Rosa had? "Don't worry, I'll give you plenty of notice when I'm ready to leave."

His expression turned even more forbidding. "I see."

She hated it when people used that catch all phrase. It made for lousy communication. For instance, what exactly did Win believe he saw and why had it put him in such a dour mood?

"There's nothing to see. I'm a responsible employee, Win. I won't leave you in the lurch."

"You said *when,* not *if.* You're already planning to leave."

He didn't need to make it sound as if she were betraying him. She was just an employee. A house-keeper…a job easy to fill again, as she was testament to. But perhaps she should tell him about her plans to get a teaching position in the fall. She discarded the idea as quickly as it came. This wasn't exactly a position with a contract and long-range career plans. She would do the job she'd been hired to do as long as she worked for Win Garrison, and she'd do it well.

And she'd give him sufficient notice to find someone else. He couldn't ask for more than that.

She did say, "I'd have to be a different person to be content with the position of cook and housekeeper for the rest of my life."

Win nodded, his face blank. "Yes. You would."

A couple of days later, Carlene was washing up the dishes left over from breakfast when Lonny came in. Once they learned she knew her way around the kitchen, Shorty no longer came up to the house to help. So, she was alone with the stable hand. She pushed the discomfort that thought caused aside. She could handle a young man like Lonny, even if he did have eyes colder than a meat locker.

Determined to take control of the encounter right from the start, she forced a smile to her lips. "If you're looking for Shorty, he's down at the stables."

"I didn't come to talk to Shorty. I came to talk to you." Lonny leaned negligently against the counter about a foot from where she stood at the sink.

She put the last plate into the bottom rack of the dishwasher and then closed it. Standing straight, she dried her hands on the kitchen towel she kept by the sink. "What can I do for you?"

Lonny's smile didn't travel from his lips to his eyes. Carlene suppressed a shiver.

"I don't want anything special," he said.

She knew he was lying. There was purpose along with unmistakable confidence in the younger man's eyes. Well, that confidence would turn to surprise if he tried anything. He would learn just as her former boss had that Carlene was not, nor would she ever be, easy prey. She was grateful that Lonny had no way of exacting the terrible price that her former principal had for her rejection. At least this time, she could say no without losing her job and her reputation in the process.

She stepped around him to pull down the platter she intended to use for lunch, using it as an excuse to move away from Lonny. She needn't have bothered. He moved with her.

"Aren't you supposed to be working right now?" she asked with no little exasperation. Really, Win could keep better track of his hands.

"You know the old saying. All work and no play makes Lonny a very dull boy and I'm anything but dull, babe."

Carlene set the platter down with more force than necessary. "My name is Carlene, not babe." She took a deep breath to recenter. "And the truth? I *am* a bit dull. I believe in working when I'm paid to work. I've got lunch to prepare and a house to clean, so if you'll excuse me."

Lonny moved forward, crowding her against the wall. He put one hand on the wall and the other on her hip, effectively caging her in. "Don't worry. I'll teach you how to have a little fun." He squeezed her hip and she pushed against his chest, but he didn't move.

Letting his gaze travel down her body, he paused at her breasts hidden behind the big white apron, before moving on. His leer sent her insides churning. She really didn't want to have to deal with this. "Although, with the way you're built, I bet you know plenty about fun, don't you, *babe?*"

His head came down as if he planned to kiss her.

Enough was enough. Some guys just didn't comprehend when a woman wasn't interested. Lonny might be young, but he was old enough to learn this lesson. She'd worn a pair of her more conservative heels today, her body too used to spending hours on heels to be comfortable in her flat sandals.

She was glad she'd done so now. Using the short, but very spiked heel of her shoe, she came down with all her weight on the top of his boot. He grunted and stumbled back a step. Before he could steady himself, she'd curled her fingers into a fist and punched him right below his ribcage just as her self-defense instructor back in Texas had taught her.

Letting out a high-pitched curse that ended on a big oof, he doubled over.

She drew herself to her full five-feet-four-inch height. "I am not anyone's babe, least of all yours. Do I make myself clear?"

He lifted his head, his arms still curved protectively around his midsection. "Yeah."

She nodded. Good. "Though I may not be old enough to be your mother, I'm certainly too old to be your anything else. I can't even be your friend because I don't offer that kind of trust to idiots who don't know any better than to make a pass at a co-worker on their boss's time."

He glared at her, but he didn't argue.

"I work for the same man you do and I expect the same respect that you give any of the other hands. Is that understood?"

He finally stood up straight, but his breathing was still a little shallow. "Understood, but you don't know what you're missing."

She let that slide. A man needed some pride, after all.

She had only one final thing to say to him. "As far as how I'm built having anything to do with my ability to have fun, I'm here to tell you that I've got all the same parts that other women do. Fun, especially the kind you appear to want, is a state of mind, not body. How I look has nothing to do with it, unless we're talking how my brain works and then maybe you'd have a clue."

Lonny nodded and sidled out of the kitchen without further comment.

Win came in the door as Lonny was leaving. "You forget what I told you to do this morning?"

Lonny shook his head. "Just needed to talk to Carlene about something."

Win looked at Carlene and then back at Lonny. "Anything I need to know about?"

Lonny's cheeks, which had taken on a slight pallor, turned red. "No, boss. Nothing important."

Win looked at Carlene. "That true?"

Carlene nodded. "It definitely wasn't anything important."

It appeared as if Win wanted to ask more questions, but Lonny was already headed toward the stables. Win stepped completely into the kitchen.

"I'm going into town to pick up some things. Do you want to come along and get groceries?"

She took longer to consider his question than she was sure he expected. She did need groceries. Rosa, the previous housekeeper, had left some things well stocked and some nearly empty. The problem was going to town with Win. She avoided him and the intensity she experienced whenever he was around as much as possible. And after her little dust-up with

Lonny, she did not want any more challenges from the male of the species.

He raised a mocking brow. "I didn't realize it would be such a difficult question."

She frowned. Why did she get the feeling that he knew exactly why she hesitated? Inexplicably, the thought stung her pride. "That would be fine, Win. Just let me get my purse."

He shrugged. "You don't need it. I'll buy the groceries."

"Don't you know that a woman feels naked without her purse?" she asked.

His eyes took on a distinctly disturbing quality and she tensed in preparation for some ribald comment, but none came. He merely said, "My sister's mentioned that a time or two."

He led her out to the car and she said, "I didn't realize that you had a sister. Does she live around here?"

Maybe Carlene had met her.

"No. She and her husband live in Portland."

Carlene settled into the passenger seat of Win's midnight-blue Ram pickup and buckled her seat belt. "Oh. What's her name?"

If he thought she was nosy, he didn't say so. He started the truck and headed toward the highway. "Leah Branson. Her husband runs Branson Consulting out of Portland. Maybe you've heard of it. They get their names in the paper from time to time."

Carlene searched her memory, but couldn't

remember ever reading about the consulting firm. "No. Sorry."

"I guess you aren't real interested in the financial section of the paper?"

She bristled at his condescending tone. "As a matter of fact, no. I like to read human interest stories, not dry articles on the state of the economy."

She also liked to read popular fiction. She'd been teased at college because of her taste in reading material, but she refused to conform to someone else's idea of what a French Literature major should want to read.

She realized she was taking easy offense again and sighed. "Sorry. I didn't mean to get defensive."

"I didn't mean to offend you, honey."

Now why didn't Win calling her honey bother her a bit when Lonny calling her babe was like nails scoring a chalkboard?

"You didn't. Not really. But just because I'm not interested in the financial section of the paper doesn't mean I'm a bimbo."

He took his gaze off the road for a few seconds to meet hers. "Does that happen often?"

"What?"

"People think you're a bimbo."

"Because I don't read the stock reports?"

"Because of how you look."

The man saw too much.

"People assume a lot of things about me based on

the way I look." She joked, "I guess it's a good thing I'm not blonde. I'd have a whole slew of assumptions made about my intelligence based on the color of my hair."

Win frowned. "Is that why you left Texas? Were too many people judging you based on your looks?"

His insight startled her and she didn't answer immediately. How much did she want to say? "You could say that," she hedged.

"I'd rather hear what you have to say about it."

"I don't like revisiting my past."

"Okay."

His easy agreement should have set her mind at rest, but she had the distinct impression that he was just biding his time. She was almost certain the subject wasn't closed as far as Win Garrison was concerned.

Looking for something besides herself to discuss, she said, "Tell me more about your sister."

His expression softened. "She's five years younger than me. She and Mark have got a couple of real cute kids."

"Where are your parents?"

His fingers gripped the steering wheel a little tighter. "I don't know where our dads are. Mom moved after each divorce and we lost touch. Neither of them were big on visitation rights."

"And your mom?" she asked.

"She died in a plane crash twelve years ago."

"Who raised your sister?"

"I did." He spoke with no inflection in his voice.

"That must have been really hard, taking on the responsibility to raise a teenage sister and losing your mom at the same time."

"Raising Leah was nothing new. Mom was too busy getting married and divorced to pay much attention to either of us. Leah was my responsibility from the day Mom brought her home from the hospital." He smiled ruefully. "I still get tied up in knots every time she cries."

His admission touched something deep inside Carlene. It was so far from something she would have expected him to say. "Divorce is incredibly traumatic for children. I can't imagine what it must have been like for you to go through two of them."

"Four."

She stared at his profile. "Your mom was married four times?"

"Five. She was divorced four times. I guess modern pop psychologists would say she had a problem with commitment."

"What happened to her fifth husband?" Carlene knew she was being unforgivably inquisitive, but she couldn't seem to help herself.

"Hank Garrison died in the plane crash with my mom."

"You use your stepfather's name. Did he adopt you?"

Win gave a harsh, bitter laugh. "Nothing so

formal. Every time Mom remarried, she insisted Leah and I take her husband's name. I had more last names growing up than pets."

"But you stuck with Garrison."

"Yeah." His terse answer didn't invite further comment.

She laid her hand on his arm. "I'm sorry."

He spared her a brief, cold glance as he pulled into a parking spot in front of the grocery store. "Save your pity. I survived."

She yanked her hand back, feeling chastised. She'd reserve her sympathy for someone who needed it, someone who had a little softness left in him. She just wished her heart didn't constrict every time she thought of Win's childhood. At least she understood the aversion to marriage he'd expressed at their first meeting. The man had a reason for distrusting the institution.

Win watched Carlene walk across the grocery store parking lot and couldn't help admiring the sway of her hips in her snug-fitting denim jeans. She looked back when she reached the front door, and waved him on impatiently. He sighed and obeyed her imperious little wave.

Pulling onto the main road, he mulled over the conversation they'd had in the car.

He didn't like talking about his mother, but he'd hoped that if he opened up to Carlene a little about his past, she'd be willing to do the same with hers. His was an open book anyway. Anything she wanted to know she could find out from one of Sunshine Spring's long time residents.

He took her curiosity as a good sign. Women wanted to know about the men they were interested in. Carlene was definitely interested in him, but she'd given a lot of mixed signals. Something was holding her back.

He had a feeling that something had happened to Carlene in Texas that left her skittish as an untried filly. He figured it was his job to help her get over her past and move on. Because he wanted her warm and willing.

CHAPTER THREE

THE next morning, Win came into the kitchen to ask Carlene a question and stopped dead in his tracks. She was bent over pulling something out of one of the low cupboards. She had the sweetest little behind he'd seen in a very long time. Hell, maybe ever. And it was positioned up in the air in a position guaranteed to turn him hard as a rock.

He took a minute just to appreciate the view.

Her jeans weren't exactly tight but they couldn't hide the sweet curve of her cheeks. He'd noticed she liked to wear her clothes loose and wondered why. Not that he minded. He didn't want the hands getting any randy ideas and he had a suspicion that Lonny already had. So far, though, the boy had done nothing overt. He just watched Carlene with hungry, hot eyes and Win didn't like it.

Along with his own randy thoughts toward the sexy little lady, Win had developed a whole passel full of possessive feelings. The only other woman he

felt this protective toward was his sister, Leah, but he
damn sure didn't want to see her naked. Now,
Carlene was another story. He figured once he got her
into his bed, he wasn't going to let her out for a good
long while.

Thinking about what he planned to spend that
time doing sent his temperature spiking. If he
wasn't careful, he was going to fantasize himself
right into a state of unrequited lust and, as much as
he wanted Carlene, he had a horse ranch and
training stables to run.

"You find what you're looking for yet?" he asked
by way of saying hello.

A muffled scream came from inside the cupboard
and she jumped. Her head must have hit something
because he heard a loud thump followed by a groan.
Shimmying backward, she got herself out of the
cupboard and turned to face him.

Her glare was as hot as his loins. "You startled
me." She made it sound as if she'd just accused him
of horse stealing.

"You didn't hear me come in?" he asked, knowing
good and well she hadn't.

She never would have remained in such a tantalizing position otherwise. When it came to desire,
Carlene acted like an untried filly. He'd seen her
looking at him with something hot in her pretty
brown eyes and that gave him hope, but she didn't
flirt or encourage him in any other way. She was like

a mare going into heat, not sure she wanted to be covered by the stallion and playing hard to get.

He'd let her dance around the corral some, but eventually he was going to corner her.

She rubbed her head, the action pressing her generous breasts against the big white apron she wore from the moment she arrived until she went home in the afternoon. "No. I didn't hear you. Why didn't you say something?"

"I did." Just not right away.

She ignored that. "Those cabinets aren't very convenient. It's almost impossible to reach the back without climbing right in."

He shrugged. "I can reach them just fine."

She went all squinty-eyed. "Well, I can't and I'm the housekeeper. Unless you want to do the cooking, you'd better find some way to make the pots and pans stored down there more accessible."

He thought about it. "Maybe I could have a pull-out shelf installed by one of the ranch hands. Would that work?"

She looked nonplussed by his easy acquiescence. "Yes. That would be fine. Terrific, in fact." Then her eyes took on a wary cast. "Not Lonny."

He narrowed his own eyes, trying to read the expression on her face. "Has he said something to you? Made you uncomfortable?"

She turned and picked up the big stew pot she'd

been after. "I'd just rather not have him underfoot. I like Shorty. Can he build the shelf?"

She set the stew pot in the sink and turned on the water.

Win didn't like dropping the subject of Lonny, but he had the impression that Carlene had said all she wanted to. Maybe she'd noticed the way Lonny looked at her too and was embarrassed by it.

With her looks, you might think she was used to that sort of male attention, but Win got the impression that she didn't like it. "Shorty's handy, but I need him in the stables right now. Call a carpenter to install the pull-out."

Turning off the water, she looked at him over her shoulder, a smile of gratitude playing on her lips. "Are you sure?"

"Honey, you can't be wondering if I can afford it." Hell, most women were only too happy to spend his money.

She laughed. "No, more wondering if you thought it was worth it. I'm glad you do. I'll call the carpenter tomorrow. Thank you."

"You're welcome."

She went to lift the cast-iron pot and water sloshed over the side. "I forgot how heavy these things are."

He sidled up behind her and put his arms around her. Taking a firm grip on the handle, he lifted it. "You want it on the stove?"

She stood still, like a rabbit caught in a snare. "Yes, please."

Her voice came out all breathy and soft. He wanted to lean down and kiss the creamy skin of her neck and see what that did to her voice, but he controlled himself. A mare couldn't be broken to bit if the handler startled her early on with demands she wasn't prepared to meet.

He stepped back, using one hand to carry the pot. He set it on the stove for her.

She turned to face him, the skin of her cheeks a rosy hue. He liked this additional evidence that his nearness had an effect on her. Standing so close to her had a pretty strong impact on him too. He'd be walking like a saddle-sore greenhorn, if he weren't careful. His usually comfortable jeans felt tight enough to do damage right now.

"Thank you."

"Anytime, honey."

She busied herself putting the stew together and he just watched. He liked the way she moved, her actions fluid and graceful. When she opened the fridge to pull out the meat, she squatted rather than bending over to get it. Amusement at the action tugged at him. If she thought the view of her thighs pressed against blue denim was any less exciting than her backside, she had a lot to learn about men.

She straightened and put the meat on the cutting block. *"What?"*

"Something the matter, honey?"

She took in a deep breath and blew it out with her eyes shut, then she opened them. "What are you doing in here? I don't think you want cooking lessons, so why are you hanging around watching me prepare dinner when you've got a stable to return to?"

Her surly tone made him grin. "You're bossy, aren't you?"

He could just about hear her teeth grinding together. "You're the one that told me you want to work uninterrupted—not have to deal with anything domestic. You must have come up to the house for a reason."

"Yeah."

"What is it?" She looked as if she'd like to wrap her fingers around his neck, but not with the intention of doing anything nice.

Why had he come up to the house? Oh, yeah. "I was wondering if you could put together a couple of casseroles for the weekend. Rosa used to do it and it helped me out a heap."

She nodded. "That won't be any problem."

"Good." He turned to leave and then stopped. "Maybe I'll put that shelf in for you myself, tomorrow."

"No, really…your idea of calling a carpenter is a good one."

"If you insist."

He left the kitchen with the look of consternation on her face fixed clearly in his mind. She noticed him all right. She hadn't look horrified, just thrown for a loop and he figured that was a good sign.

He'd break that filly to bridle, but first he had to get her used to having him around. Then he'd work on the touching.

Just like a nervous mare and he had a real special touch with nervous fillies, just ask anyone.

Carlene was ready to quit her job as Win's housekeeper two weeks later. Between Lonny's glares and Win's bedroom eyes, she was at her wit's end.

Win never implied that her job was even slightly reliant on her sleeping with him, but then again he made no bones about the fact that he wanted her in his bed. He hadn't actually come out and said so, but he watched her with a hot gaze that made her insides melt. It didn't help that he found more excuses than a student with spring fever did to skip class, to get close to her.

Just yesterday he had insisted on helping her get a large ceramic bowl down from the top shelf in the pantry. That would have been fine except that he didn't allow her to move out of the way before his strong, masculine body was stretching up and leaning over her to reach the bowl. Again, no problem.

Except that the effect Win's closeness had on her senses couldn't be denied. She'd forgotten for one full minute what she'd been planning to do and just stood there, breathing in his scent. He'd noticed.

Darn him. And he'd laughed. No doubt he thought she was like a plump peach, ripe and ready to be picked off the tree.

She sighed and cut some more shortening into the flour for the biscuits she was preparing to go with dinner.

She didn't want to quit.

She liked her new job. Shorty might not know much about cooking, but he was a sweetheart. She liked the rest of the ranch hands as well…except Lonny. She enjoyed cooking for them and Win was a tidy person. Keeping his house clean was a cinch, especially with the help of maid service that came in three times a week. Mondays and Wednesdays and once on the weekend.

She liked everything about working at the Bar G except the way its owner made her feel.

Dealing with an interested male shouldn't be so difficult. Men had been interested in her since she started wearing a bra, but Win was different. She had an almost overwhelming desire to give in to the invitation she saw in his eyes and that scared her spitless. He'd made it very clear that he wasn't interested in marriage and she hadn't changed her mind about an affair. First, because she believed that she deserved more than that and second, because no school board for a small town like Sunshine Springs was going to hire a teacher with a reputation for loose morals. Gossip always got around.

Awareness skittered down her spine and she spun around, dropping the pastry cutter into the ceramic bowl with a clang.

Win leaned against the wall watching her. He did a lot of that, leaning against a wall or something and just watching her. It made her nervous and hot and jittery besides, something she definitely didn't want to deal with.

She forced a smile to her lips. "Hi."

He pushed away from the wall and walked toward her. She started getting nervous again as the distance between them closed to less than a few inches.

She backed up, but ran into the counter behind her. "Win?"

He reached out and brushed her cheek. "I thought the flour was for the biscuits."

"It is." She couldn't think of anything else to say. She couldn't seem to move away either.

"It's not real attractive makeup, but on you it's kinda cute."

"No." Then understanding dawned. She whipped her hands up and scrubbed at her cheeks, getting rid of any remaining flour Win hadn't brushed away with his hand. "I didn't realize I was wearing dinner."

"I wouldn't mind," he said.

"What?" Was it just that his proximity had scrambled her brains, or was he really not making any sense?

His voice dropped to a husky drawl. "I wouldn't mind you wearing my dinner."

As the words registered Carlene felt her blood spike with both anger and desire. She forced the anger to the forefront. Placing her hands on Win's chest, she shoved. Hard. He fell back a couple of paces.

She untied the big white apron she wore to protect her clothes with jerky movements. She yanked it off and tossed it on the table. "That's it. I quit."

When Win didn't say anything, particularly, "I'm sorry and won't you please stay?" she reached her hand out and poked him in the chest with her forefinger. "Listen here, Mr Bedroom Eyes. I've had my fill of you watching me like I'm a mare in heat and you're the stallion sent to cover me. Do you understand me?"

His smile infuriated her. "I think so."

She crossed her arms over her chest and glared at him. "Just what do you understand?"

"You don't want me to look at you like I want you."

"Well?" she asked.

"Well, what?"

She blew out an exasperated breath. "Are you going to stop?"

He reached out and brushed his fingers down her arm. Desire pooled in her lower belly and she bit back a groan. "I don't know if I can. I do want you, Carlene. I'm not real sure why that bothers you so much. I haven't pushed you to do anything about it, have I?"

She had to give him that. "No. You haven't, but that's not the point."

"What is the point? You don't like feeling like you want me too? I can fix that for you, honey."

The promise in his voice made her shiver with feelings she did not want to acknowledge or give in to. "Forget it. I'm not interested in a one-night stand and that's all you're offering, isn't it, Win? You don't want marriage or commitment."

His fingers curled around her upper arm. "I made my feelings on marriage plain the day I interviewed you, but there's a whole lot of ground between a one-night stand and marriage. I never said I wasn't interested in any kind of commitment. I can guarantee you that while you share my bed, no one else will."

"An affair?" Outrage burned through her and she twisted from his grasp. "You think a no-strings, open ended affair is an appreciable improvement over a one-night stand?"

His eyes narrowed. "You aren't going to convince me that you've married every man you've slept with."

The warmth of desire she had been feeling shifted to a frozen sort of pain. Win was like all the others, making assumptions based on how she looked and not who she was. Wouldn't he just die laughing if he found out that she was a twenty-six-year-old virgin? She might look like a pinup in a girlie calendar, but she'd fought against the image her entire life.

She dated very little, in high school because she had been more interested in her studies than in boys and in college because once the men she dated figured out that she didn't put out, they went looking for greener pastures. She had planned to change her innocent status a while ago with Grant Strickland, a truly nice man.

She had decided the time had come. Unfortunately, or fortunately, depending on how you looked at it, her timing had been off. Grant had been in love with another woman and hadn't been interested. She still felt the heat of embarrassment when she considered how she'd thrown herself at the man. She had truly lousy instincts when it came to men she was attracted to.

And Win was no exception. Their situation made her want to cry. He affected her as no other man ever had, including Grant, but she wasn't willing to risk her reputation and her goals for something as transitory as an affair, especially an affair with a man who made it clear that long-term commitment would never be an option.

She moved to the door.

She couldn't stay here. She wanted Win too much. The risk was too great. Grabbing her purse from the broom cupboard, she said, "You can send my check in the mail."

She had to get out of there before her resolve to keep a lid on her emotions faltered.

Her hand was on the knob to open the door when his fingers clamped around her wrist in a vicelike grip.

* * *

Win knew he couldn't let Carlene walk out that door. He didn't get what she was so upset about, but he was going to find out. They were attracted to each other. That was not a bad thing. At least, not to his way of thinking.

He kept his fingers locked firmly around her wrist as he pulled her around to face him. "What the hell do you think you are doing?"

She looked at him as if he'd lost a few marbles. "I'm leaving. Now, let go of my arm."

"No. I'm not letting go of you and you aren't leaving." He leaned forward until his face was close enough to hers that their breath mingled. "Do I make myself clear?"

She glared at him and said, "Yes," between clenched teeth.

He leaned back a little, but didn't let go of her wrist. "We're going to talk this out."

The stubborn woman shook her head at him. Didn't she know that women were supposed to want to talk things out?

"We have nothing to discuss. You want a convenient sex object for your housekeeper. Only you neglected to mention that as part of my job description. I'm wondering why though…you were quick enough to tell me your no marriage policy. I am not interested in being *anyone's* temporary squeeze, so I'm leaving."

Sex object? Temporary squeeze? Putting a tight

lid on his temper, he hooked one hand under her knees and the other behind her back. She screeched something about overbearing, insufferable cowboys, when he picked her up. He ignored her. The powder keg that was his temper was liable to go off if he paid attention.

She kept up a litany of complaints all the way out of the kitchen, through the courtyard, and into his living room. She was shoving at his chest with her fists by the time he dropped her gently onto the couch.

She shot right back up again and stood toe to toe with him, her eyes shooting sparks. "You cannot treat your employees this way and expect them to stay. What did you do, manhandle Rosa until she left?"

The thought of anyone manhandling the two-hundred-and-fifty-pound Mexican grandmother of twelve surprised a smile out of him. "No. Rosa left because her daughter went into early labor with baby number four."

When Carlene just scowled at him, he sighed and shoveled his fingers through his hair. "Damn it. I didn't mean to manhandle you either, honey."

"Don't call me honey. Employees take just as dim a view of being referred to in a too familiar fashion as they do to being manhandled."

"Will you be reasonable? I didn't manhandle you."

Her eyebrows shot up. "What would you call carrying me through the house against my will?"

"Trying to get you someplace where we weren't

going to be interrupted by Shorty or one of the other hands," he was goaded into shouting.

She settled her hands on her shapely hips. "What's wrong with Shorty overhearing me quit? It's not like a state secret or something."

He'd about had all the sass he was going to take off of her, but he tried once more to discuss the situation rationally. "You aren't going to quit. I didn't want Shorty, or anyone else, listening to us discuss our *relationship*."

Her toe started tapping and he actually moved his booted foot back a couple of inches, to get it out of range, before he realized what he was doing.

"We don't have a relationship except that of an employer and employee. As far as I'm concerned, that one is over."

"Fine. Quit your job as my housekeeper, but don't expect that to end it."

Her eyes narrowed. "Are you threatening me? What do you plan to do? Stalk me?"

That did it. He'd reached his limit. She seemed to realize it as soon as he had because she tensed, ready to run. He didn't give her the chance. Grabbing her arms, he yanked her up against him and slammed his mouth down on hers.

The only problem was that the moment his lips touched hers, all his anger evaporated and was replaced by raging desire.

* * *

Carlene could have remained an unwilling partici-
pant in Win's passionate assault if he'd stayed angry.
He didn't. The grip he had on her arms, which hadn't
been that fierce to begin with, loosened. He reached
up and unclipped the barrette she'd been using to
hold her hair back and tunneled his fingers into the
unruly curls.

Suddenly their argument…her fury…everything
but the feel of Win's lips on hers ceased to exist. She
allowed her hands, which had been fisted against his
shirtfront, to relax against him. His muscles felt solid
under the soft fabric of his shirt.

His lips moved over hers, softly, coaxingly. He
licked her bottom lip and she shivered.

"Open for me, honey. I'm desperate to taste you."

She couldn't deny the agonized need she heard in
his voice. Allowing her lips to part, she silently invited
Win in. He didn't need any urging. His tongue swept
inside and took complete dominion of her mouth.

Feelings that she'd never experienced roared to
life inside Carlene and she clung to Win, afraid that
if she didn't she would fall down.

He groaned and pulled her close against his body,
cupping her backside with one strong hand and
locking his other hand behind her head, tangling it
in her hair.

She allowed her hands to trail up his neck and
twined her fingers together once her hands were firmly
anchored behind his head. His tongue demanded a

response in her mouth and she eagerly gave it. She met him thrust for thrust and reveled in the sound of hungry need he emitted.

Using the hand on her bottom, he rocked her pelvis against his and an electric current shot through her feminine core. Heat and dampness grew between her legs. She whimpered and he broke his mouth away from hers to trail kisses down her neck and up again toward her ear. Her breath came rushing out on a high-pitched wail. It just felt so good, better than anything she'd ever known.

"Oh, yes, baby, just like that."

His husky voice grated against her ear and his hot breath made her shiver uncontrollably. Suddenly the world tilted and she found herself lying under Win on the leather sofa.

Her world had shrunk down to the soft cushions at her back and the hard man lying on top of her.

"We're going to be so good together, honey. I promise."

His words broke through the passionate daze she had slipped into and she started to struggle. "Let me up, Win."

He didn't seem to hear her as he unbuttoned the top three buttons on her blouse in quick succession. He slipped his hand inside and the feel of his fingers on her aching flesh almost sent her spinning back toward the passion filled no man's land she'd been caught up in since Win's lips had first touched hers.

His next words acted like a cold shower on her senses, however. "Don't worry, honey, I've got a condom."

She started to struggle in earnest. "Let me up. I mean it, Win. Let me go."

He stopped kissing her and lifted his head to stare into her eyes. "What?"

"Please, let me go." Foolish tears gathered in the corner of her eyes.

Win slowly moved off of her body, his expression wary, and then pulled her into a sitting position next to him. "I was going too fast, wasn't I?"

She nodded, unable to speak past the frustrated tears clogging her throat. He no doubt now believed he had all the evidence he needed that she was exactly what he thought, a woman willing to share a no-strings affair. Her fingers trembled as she tried to rebutton her blouse. She muttered an expletive when they slipped for the third time off the button.

Win brushed her fingers out of the way. "Let me do that."

He had her buttoned up in less than ten seconds. The man was fast, about a lot of things. He tipped her chin up so that she had to meet his gaze. His blue eyes had grown dark and in them she could see the remnants of the wanting he'd been forced to control.

"Okay now?" he asked.

She'd never be okay again. "Yes," she nevertheless said.

He nodded. He turned and brushed around the floor with his fingers. "Got it."

He held up her barrette as if it were first prize on the show circuit.

She took it from him and managed to clip her hair into some semblance of order. "Thank you."

"Any time, honey."

She took a deep breath and let it out slowly, praying for strength as she did so. "We need to talk, Win."

He nodded, his expression serious. "I know."

The problem was, she didn't know what to say.

He saved her from having to come up with the right words by speaking first. "I owe you an apology." He pushed his fingers through his hair. "Hell, honey, I'm not used to the feelings you bring out in me. My only excuse is that when you threatened to leave, I knew I had to do something to stop you. Picking you up and bringing you in here seemed like the most straightforward approach to keeping you around."

She smiled at his explanation. "What were you planning to do tomorrow when I didn't show up for work? Kidnap me?"

She meant it as a joke, but he took her seriously. His face took on a pained expression. "I didn't get that far in my thinking. I guess this he-man stuff only takes a guy so far, huh?"

A guy who understood the word no. Earlier

evidence to the contrary, she had a strong feeling that Win was one of those men. "Yes."

He nodded. "What are you going to do?"

CHAPTER FOUR

THE question surprised Carlene. She would have assumed that after the way she responded to his kiss, Win would think he had her full cooperation in his plans for an affair. Surprisingly, it was his doubt that precipitated her own. If he'd gone on demanding that she stay, she would have been able to walk out.

"I don't know," she answered.

"Would you stay if I promised to take things at your pace?"

The offer threw her. She didn't want to set the pace to an affair and yet she couldn't bring herself to throw the offer back in Win's face. She didn't doubt it had taken a toll on his pride to make it. He was not a man used to women saying no…or letting anyone else be in control. She decided honesty was the only alternative.

"I'm attracted to you."

He smiled. "I could tell."

She swallowed. "Yes. Well. Although I find you

more attractive than any man I've ever met, I'm not interested in an affair. I'm too old to play those games."

Instead of the angry frown she expected, he smiled. "What are you? Twenty-four, twenty-five? You're not exactly at the age when most women's biological clocks start ticking."

"I'm twenty-six and it isn't my biological clock I'm worried about. At the risk of sounding hopelessly old-fashioned, it's my reputation." And her heart, but she didn't think she needed to admit that right now.

He stared at her for several taut moments, as if testing the strength of her will. Finally, he nodded. "I can't say that the idea of sneaking around thrills me, but I can understand your desire to be discreet."

In for a penny, in for a pound, her mother had always said. "Discreet isn't what I was thinking about exactly. I meant it when I said I didn't want to have an affair."

His hands flexed, then fisted against his thighs. "Are you saying that the kiss we just shared didn't change your mind?"

She nodded, feeling miserable. "That's exactly what I'm saying. I'm not going to pretend that I don't want you, Win."

He gave a harsh laugh. "Thanks for that much at least."

"But, I'm not in the market for a no-strings affair."

"Are you really going to quit?"

She sighed. She didn't want to, now more than

ever. "No. I'm a big girl and I can handle a little sexual attraction."

She hoped and prayed with all her heart that was true. She needed this job and the thought of never seeing Win again went through her soul like an arctic wind. It might not be the safest course of action, but it was the only one she could live with.

He gave her a slow sexy wink, his relief evident. "I can too, honey, but I'm telling you right now that I want you and that isn't going to change either."

She nodded, accepting his statement for what it was—a challenge. She just hoped she wasn't being irreparably stupid in believing she could meet it.

"So is it true you carried Carlene through the house like a sack of potatoes yesterday?"

Shorty's questions caught Win by surprise and he damn near yanked on the bridle of the horse he was leading. His head shot up and he met the older man's gaze. "Where'd you hear a fool story like that?"

He'd never carried a sack of potatoes cradled in his arms in his life.

"Joe said he came into the kitchen looking for a leftover piece of pie just as you were carrying our new cook to parts unknown." Shorty stopped and adjusted his hat back on his head. "Said Carlene was yelling her head off."

Win would have to teach Joe a lesson about gossip. He didn't much like the thought of his hands discussing him and Carlene, but he was smart enough to realize he probably couldn't stop it. "He said that, did he?"

Shorty hooked his thumb in his belt. "Yeah. We was all pretty sure the little lady was gonna quit. No one was looking forward to going back to my vittles, I can tell ya."

"She didn't quit." Win was still a little surprised and very pleased by that fact.

"Uh, huh. I noticed. She's in there making lasagna for dinner tonight." Shorty rubbed his stomach in appreciation. "Makes a man relish working up an appetite for the kind of cookin' *that* little lady provides."

Win figured there was a point to this conversation, so he remained silent, waiting for Shorty to get to it.

"A gal like that needs a hand gentle on the leads, boss."

Win wasn't surprised by the warning. Carlene had won the hearts of his hands within a couple of days of her arrival. It wasn't just her cooking either. She had a ready smile and kind word for just about everyone.

Everyone except Lonny.

Win still didn't know what had happened that day he'd come upon Lonny leaving the kitchen with the expression of a newly branded calf on his face. He could guess though and it irritated the hell out of Win that another man felt he had a right to make a pass at Carlene. The way she'd acted about having Lonny make the shelf in the kitchen had made him even more suspicious, but until he knew for sure he couldn't feed the other man his teeth.

Win wanted his hands and the rest of the world to know that Carlene was his woman. Only she wasn't his woman, not yet anyway. And when she finally gave in, he had an ugly feeling the woman was going to want to be "discreet".

He didn't know what women thought they were gaining by hiding a relationship, but he figured she wasn't going to back down real easy on that point. Hell, nothing said she'd back down about getting involved either. Nothing, but the way she responded to his touch.

A man could find a lot of hope in having a woman respond to him the way Carlene responded to Win.

Shorty cleared his throat, reminding Win that he wasn't alone with his thoughts.

"You know what I mean, boss?"

What had the man said? Oh, yeah, something about a gentle hand on the leads. "Carlene's not a horse, Shorty," he said, ignoring the fact that he'd used similar comparisons himself in his own mind.

Shorty shrugged. "Women and horses got a lot in common. They don't take kindly to rough treatment and you've gotta coax 'em into trusting you."

"Where'd you learn that? The cowboy school for seduction?"

"I was married a heap o' years, boy, and a man learns something about women living with one day in and day out."

Win wouldn't argue that. Living with his mom for eighteen years and his wife for less than two had taught him plenty about the opposite sex, the most important lesson being that they didn't stick around. From what Carlene had said about moving on the first day she'd come to work for him, he figured she'd follow the same pattern. But he'd damn well have her in his bed before that happened.

"Will it make you feel better to know that I apologized?"

Shorty's eyes widened and then his wrinkled face split in a grin. "She's got you apologizing already, boss? Now that's a good sign, a mighty good sign."

"I'd appreciate it if you and the rest of the hands would leave off speculating on my relationship with Carlene."

Chuckling, Shorty pulled his hat back down over his brow. "Didn't realize you two was already at the *relationship* stage. Lonny ain't going to like hearing that."

Win frowned. "If Lonny's smart, he'll keep his opinions on the matter to himself."

"Oh, he ain't stupid, boss. Don't figure he'll say anything, but don't know that he's gonna give up on Carlene either. I've seen the way he watches her. He's got ideas, that's for sure."

Win watched Carlene with wanting in his eyes too, but what he wanted from Carlene and what that young punk that worked for him wanted were very different things. Weren't they? *Hell, yes,* he told himself. He wanted more than a quick toss in the sheets. He wanted Carlene for as long as it took to work out whatever it was they had going between them.

He figured Lonny was just looking for some experience with a beautiful woman. Well, he wasn't going to get it with Carlene. Win toyed with the thought of firing the young stable hand, but decided that in all fairness he couldn't fire the boy for having feelings. At least not today.

A warning might be in order though. Win scowled at Shorty. "If he wants to keep his job, he'll keep his hormones under control when he's around Carlene."

Satisfaction settled over Shorty's features. "It's like that, is it? Glad to see that you ain't so blind after all. Women like Carlene don't come along in a man's life every day, you know? 'Bout time you settled down and had yourself a family. Carlene'll make a mighty fine mother, if you ask me."

Win's scowl deepened. "You can forget any pipedreams about marriage, old man. The only kids I need around are my sister's. I see them when she visits and then she takes them home, just the way I like."

An empty feeling in his gut belied Win's words, but he refused to withdraw them.

Shorty snorted in disgust. "Thought you was finally smartening up, boss. Guess you ain't." His gaze slid toward the house where Carlene stood beating rugs in the spring sun. "Then again, maybe there's hope for you yet."

"Don't count on it," Win replied.

Shorty turned and walked away, muttering about mule-headed horses' asses that passed for men.

Win watched Shorty's retreating figure, his thoughts in turmoil, and it was all Carlene's fault. She had him so twisted in knots he didn't know if he was coming or going. One thing he did know—he wasn't going to give up a lifetime of hard-learned lessons for any woman, even one as appealing as his housekeeper.

She acted like a woman who was looking for marriage, but Win didn't buy it. She'd already made it clear that she was moving on. She wasn't really interested in permanence either. So why was she so bothered with the idea of an affair? She was bringing up marriage as some sort of barrier between them.

He didn't know why she felt as if she needed one, but he'd find out. Once he did, he'd overcome it and any others she planned to erect. After all, he was a man that knew how to get what he wanted and he wanted Carlene Daniels.

A week later, he wasn't one step closer to breaching Carlene's defenses. In fact, he felt as if she built a better corral to keep in her emotions than the one he used to exercise his horses. The woman was as stubborn and frustrating as they came.

He sighed and leaned back in his chair, putting his booted feet up on the table. Satisfaction that no one was there to scold settled over him. Now if he were a married man, he'd have to listen to some woman reprimand him for putting his boots on the furniture, even the outside furniture.

When his ex-wife wasn't complaining about the lack of social life and opportunities in Sunshine Springs, she had nagged Win about his manners, or lack thereof. She found his cowboy ways too earthy for her delicate tastes. Too bad she hadn't figured that out *before* marrying him. Too bad he hadn't figured it out either. There had been some clues, but his judgment had been clouded by fear, grief and unsatisfied lust.

Rachel had insisted on waiting to go to bed together until they got married.

As far as he could see, she'd used sex and anything else that came handy to try to manipulate him, first into marriage and then into selling the Bar G and Garrison Stables so they could move to the city. He'd learned a lot in his short association with Rachel, that was for sure. Lessons he wasn't about to ignore.

Thoughts of his ex-wife always put him in a bad mood, so he welcomed the interruption of a ringing doorbell. He stood up and headed toward the front of the house, thinking of Carlene when the chimes rang out a second time before he had a chance to open the door.

When he finally opened it, however, it wasn't Carlene standing on the other side. It was his baby sister. He felt guilty almost immediately for the sense of disappointment he had to squelch.

Leah threw herself in his arms. "Win, you've got to help me. I don't know what to do anymore. It's just too much," she said between broken sobs against his shirtfront.

He patted her back and looked past her to the small compact parked near the front of his house. In the fading light, he could make out the outline of two tiny heads, but no other adult. She'd brought Win's four-year-old niece and two-year-old nephew, but her husband, Mark, hadn't accompanied her.

He hugged his sister and then set her away from him. "Hush, Leah. Let's get the kids inside and then you can tell me all about what's bothering you."

She nodded, swallowing a sob. Shoot. He hated it when she cried. His insides twisted like the strands of a lariat.

It wasn't any surprise that an hour later he found himself agreeing to keep the kids for a few days while Leah tried to get her head on straight. She needed a break and it sounded as if her marriage was on the skids.

He sure hoped Carlene liked children because her job description was about to change. He needed a nanny as well as a housekeeper. Hell, he'd give her a raise—that should help get her to agree.

Especially when he told her the other change he needed her to make.

* * *

"Move in here? Are you nuts?" Carlene stared at him, her eyes clearly showing every bit of what she was thinking for the first time that week. The little woman was furious. "I took this job expecting to clean house and cook. Now you want a live-in nanny? No way, Win. I'm not doing it. You'll have to find someone else."

He had to convince her and soon. He had a full day of work ahead of him and he was already a couple of hours behind, having had to wait to leave the house until Carlene showed up.

"I told you when I interviewed you, it's your job to deal with the domestic stuff." He smiled in what he hoped was a coaxing manner. "I know taking care of the kids is above and beyond what I hired you to do, but it's not permanent and I'll give you a big bonus."

She erupted all over him like Mt. St. Helens, bristling with outrage as she drew herself up. "You think you can *bribe* me to put my reputation on the line, not to mention exhaust myself caring for two toddlers?"

He didn't know what her fixation with her reputation was, but she must know something about children if she knew taking care of a couple of toddlers was so tiring. He had to agree. Shelly had woken in the night calling for her mom. It had been all Win could do to get the little girl to go back to sleep. He didn't look forward to more nights of the same. Children needed a woman's touch. Carlene talked as if she'd had personal experience along those lines.

"You taken care of a lot of kids?"

She eyed him warily, but nodded. "I babysat all through high school. I started watching one set of twins the year they were born and helped their mom potty-train them before I went off to college. I have no doubt your sister needs a break, especially if her husband travels so much, but you agreeing to give her that break does not make it my responsibility."

He opened his mouth to answer and she forestalled him. "You're going to have to find someone else."

He frowned, starting to get a little annoyed. He didn't think a woman as kind as Carlene would be so difficult to convince to help him. Didn't she fall all over herself mixing herbal teas for Shorty's arthritis? Hadn't she refused to let him fire Lonny when Win had finally cornered her about the scene in the kitchen?

He'd think that kindness and understanding would extend to her boss as well. "Well, your job description just got changed. Now it includes watching my sister's children while I'm busy at the stables."

"Hire a teenager to help you," she shot back.

"Don't know any well enough to trust my sister's children into their care."

That seemed to stymie her. Her mouth, which had been open, ready to level another sally at him, closed with a snap.

Before she could marshal her thoughts, he went in for the kill. "Come on, honey. It's only for a few days. Don't tell me that you can turn your back on two defenseless little kids that need you."

A frown wiped the expression of thoughtful concern she had been wearing right off her face. "I'm not turning my back on 'two defenseless little children'. I'm refusing to do what their overbearing, arrogant, thickheaded uncle is demanding I do. There's a big difference in my mind."

"That 'overbearing, arrogant, thickheaded' man is also your boss and like I reminded you…it's your job to take care of the domestic stuff. You want help with the kids? Call a service to send someone to help you with the cooking and other household stuff, but I'm not leaving my niece and nephew under the responsibility of a stranger. I want *you* with them. Just for this little bit," he reiterated.

"Win! *You're* the one that told your sister you would take care of her kids."

The pocket spitfire was stubborn, he'd give her that, but he wasn't giving in on this. He couldn't. He had too much going on both with the free range horses and the stables to take time off right now. "Rosa would have done it, no problem. She would have insisted."

Carlene looked like a tea kettle ready to whistle. "And that matters to me why?"

"Because she was a good housekeeper and you are too."

Laughter burst from the woman in front of him.

"You think I aspire to golden-star status as a house-keeper?"

"You are the kind of person who takes pride in doing her job to the best of her ability, no matter what that job is."

"I've been a great housekeeper for you."

"And now I'm asking you for something extra. No different than asking Shorty to stay with a foaling mare or myself to get up two hours early for a month to take an extra training project on." He took a breath, thought of saying something else and then sighed. "Please, Carlene. I need your help."

The starch went right out of her as he said the final words and he wondered why he hadn't thought to use that approach before. Mostly his pride. He hated saying please or admitting he needed anything from anybody, but especially a woman. He'd been let down too many times.

"Okay. I'll work something out, but not the nights. You're going to have to handle those on your own."

"As far as caring for the children, that's not a problem, but I've got mares ready to foal. If I'm needed in the stable at night, I can't leave Shelly and Jared in the house alone. Besides, they're going to miss their mama something fierce. They'll need comforting. A woman's touch."

"I don't see how a perfect stranger could comfort them any better than their uncle."

That made his lips twitch. Was she really that

ignorant of the effect she had on people? "Honey, you could comfort a wounded lion cub. Shelly and Jared are going to love you."

Her cheeks turned an interesting shade of pink. "Thank you, but don't think that flattery is going to win this argument."

He didn't. He figured Carlene's soft heart could do that for him. He heard a noise come through the door he'd left open to the courtyard. His spirits lifted. The kids were awake. He knew Carlene wouldn't stay stubborn on the issue of staying the nights once she'd met Jared and Shelly. They were great kids.

"Can you at least stay tonight?"

"Yes." She fixed him with a steely stare. "But just this one night. Got it?"

He smiled. He had it all right and he had her. After the first night of holding Shelly when she woke up calling for her mommy, Carlene would be hooked. She'd see the kids needed her. If having her stay the nights made her that much more accessible to him, well, a smart man knew when to take advantage of his good fortune.

Another noise came, this one a tad louder.

Carlene's head shot up. "One of them is awake."

"Sounds like Jared. He's probably hungry for some breakfast. Why don't you rustle up something? I'll go get him."

He left Carlene staring after him with a pretty darn adorable look of confusion on her face.

He had been right. Jared was awake and standing in the playpen that Leah had brought with her. His baby-fine blond hair stuck to the side of his head. He stopped crying and smiled when Win entered the room. Chubby little arms reached up from the playpen. "Up, Unca Win, up."

Win obliged willingly, letting his gaze shift to the sofa where his niece still slept. He'd put the kids in the study because all the bedrooms were on the upper levels, he'd move them to the bedroom when they were asleep. He carried Jared to the floor and saw about changing the little guy's clothes. By the time he was finished, Shelly had woken up.

She knelt in the middle of the sofa that looked a whole lot bigger under her than when he sat on it and rubbed sleep from her eyes. "Uncle Win, where's Mommy?"

Win scooped Jared off the dresser and used his free arm to pick up Shelly. He carried them out the door and through the courtyard toward the kitchen. "Your mommy let me have you two for company for a few days. You know how lonely Uncle Win gets when you aren't around."

Shelly contemplated Win, her gaze serious as only a four-year-old's could be. "Mommy said she needed a break. She was crying. Is she done crying, Uncle Win?"

Pain lanced through Win at the question. Shelly had seen too much of Leah's unhappiness.

He carried her and Jared through the kitchen door. "Yeah, sweetpea, I think she's done crying, except for maybe a little because she misses you."

"Uncle Win."

He set the kids down at the table and knelt down to Shelly's eye level. "Yeah, sweetpea?"

Shelly's lower lip trembled and her baby-soft brown eyes filled with moisture. "I want my mommy."

Hell.

Carlene stepped forward. Her smile was bright enough to light a stadium. "Good morning. You must be Shelly. I'm Carlene. You know, sometimes I want my mom too."

Win watched his niece's eyes widen. "You do?"

Carlene nodded, her expression sincere. "You bet. She lives in Texas. That's a long way from here. When I miss her, I try to do things I like to do with her so I won't miss her so much. Do you think that would work for you?"

Shelly pursed her lips in thought, but she'd stopped crying. "I don't know."

"What do you like to do with your mom?"

"I like it when she rocks me and reads me a story. Mostly she holds both me and Jared," Shelly said.

Carlene nodded with enthusiasm as if Shelly had just revealed the secret to eternal youth. "You know, I like to rock little children and read to them too.

Maybe you'd let me rock you and Jared—what do you think?"

A little of Shelly's unhappiness faded from her eyes. "I guess."

Carlene smiled that thousand-watt smile again. "Okay. What do you say we have some breakfast first?"

"I's hungry," announced Jared. "I's wants beck-fast."

Carlene and Shelly both giggled and Win relaxed. Everything was going to be just fine. He met Carlene's eyes over the top of Shelly's head and mouthed a "thank you". She shrugged and returned to cooking pancakes.

He walked over to her and kissed her softly on the temple in gratitude. "Thank you. You're one in a million, honey."

She turned startled eyes to him, her lips soft and inviting. The only thing that stopped him from accepting that invitation was the presence of the two little people at the table. They stared at Win and Carlene with identical looks of interest on their faces. He sighed. Another time.

CHAPTER FIVE

CARLENE tossed her cotton nightgown in the overnight bag along with clothes for the next day.

Taking advantage of the fact that she had managed to get both Jared and Shelly to take an afternoon nap, she had left Shorty in charge and rushed to her apartment to pack for her overnight at Win's. She didn't want the children to wake up while she was gone, although she couldn't have said why. They undoubtedly knew Shorty much better than they knew her, but she felt the need to be there in case they woke wanting their mom.

She made quick work of her packing and was back in her car in a matter of minutes. She flipped on the air-conditioning. Summer in Oregon's desert wasn't as scorching as west Texas, but it was hot enough. She breathed an air of relief as the refrigerated air from the vents cooled her skin.

If only she could cool her reaction to Win as easily. She'd fought him over watching his niece and nephew not because she truly had a problem with taking care of the children, but because she didn't want another link between herself and Win. She felt the strings tying her to her sexy boss tightening each day. His desire beat at her whenever they were in the same room together and that wouldn't be so bad if there weren't a corresponding cadence inside of her.

There hadn't been another incident like the one when he'd kissed her until she'd forgotten common sense. Win had been a perfect gentleman, but that didn't alleviate the pressure she felt. She got the sense that Win was just biding his time until she surrendered to the feelings between them. He seemed to think that them making love was a foregone conclusion.

The thing that terrified her was that she was beginning to wonder if he was right.

She went to sleep every night with his image fixed firmly in her mind and woke up each morning anticipating seeing him again. His prominence in her thoughts both scared and exhilarated her. She'd never felt this drawn to another man, not even Grant. She wanted Win, but she wanted more than a short-term affair.

She wanted it all and Win acted as if marriage was one step away from maximum-security prison. She sighed. Was it any wonder that she was scared? Well, one thing was for certain. She wasn't going to stay the nights at Win's after tonight. He'd have to find someone else.

Despite its celebrity part-time residents, Sunshine Springs was a small town with small-town attitudes. She wasn't about to risk her prospects of getting hired as a teacher again by living with Win. It didn't matter if she slept with him or not, plenty of people would take it as a foregone conclusion. Look at the way the principal at the grade school Zoe taught at had reacted to her living with Grant. Grant had been Zoe's best friend for pretty much all of her life too. Tyler had told Carlene all about it and she knew better than to push her own luck.

High-school teachers got just as much, if not more, scrutiny. Especially one with her track record.

She pulled her car to a stop near Win's house. It would make the perfect house for a family.

A sudden image of a little boy with Win's startling blue eyes and black hair playing in the courtyard fountain took her breath away. More staggering than the vision of the little boy playing in the pond was the absolute certainty that the child belonged to both *her* and Win. It seemed so real that she was surprised to realize that she hadn't yet gotten out.

She shook her head ruefully and stepped out of her car. The heat was doing things to her brain, that or the knowledge that she was tempted to chuck all her requirements out the window and give herself to Win, no commitments.

Making a baby with Win would be fairly easy.

Making a family with the man would be another matter entirely.

The cry woke Carlene from a fitful sleep. She sat straight up in bed and tried desperately to make sense of the shadowy images she could barely make out in the darkness. This wasn't her bed. This wasn't her room in her cozy little apartment either.

Another cry rent the air. *"Mommy!"*

Everything crystallized in Carlene's brain. She was sleeping in the guest room next to Shelly and Jared's. When the cry was followed by audible sobs, she jumped out of bed. Taking no time to put on a bathrobe, she rushed from the room. *Where was Win?* Couldn't he hear Shelly's heart-rending cries? Carlene stepped on a toy and let out a squeak as she stumbled into the children's room.

The night-light that Win had put in at Shelly's request illuminated the distraught little girl sitting in the center of the double bed. Carlene didn't hesitate. She put her arms out and Shelly flew into them.

Locking her arms around Carlene's neck, Shelly choked out words between her tears. "I'm s-scared. I want my mommy."

Carlene hugged the little girl fiercely. "Shh, sugar-bear. It's going to be okay."

Continuing to speak softly to Shelly, Carlene crossed to the rocking-chair in the corner of the room. It was a roomy, old-fashioned wooden rocker; the kind Carlene's mom had used to rock her when she woke scared in the night. She sat down and cradled Shelly on her lap. Rubbing the little girl's back, Carlene continued to speak comforting words and rocked the chair in a soothing motion until Shelly's crying subsided.

She didn't stop rocking until Shelly's limp posture and deep breathing indicated she had once again fallen asleep. Even then, Carlene stayed in the chair, holding the child. The feel of the small body tucked against hers filled Carlene with longing. Win said she was too young to be worried about her biological clock, but what about her heart's desires?

Stifling a sigh, she stood up. Carlene put Shelly back into the bed, tucking the covers around her small form. She turned and checked on Jared, surprised he had slept through his sister's upset. His blanket had slipped down and Carlene pulled it up to cover him before turning to leave the room.

She stepped into the hall and stifled a scream as a shadow unattached itself from the wall and came toward her. *"Win."*

"Is she okay?"

Carlene nodded, her heart beating too frantically for her to form a proper response.

He had obviously come straight from bed. His hair was disheveled as if he'd recently run his fingers through it. He hadn't bothered to put on a shirt or shoes and the top button on his Levis was undone. Her fingers itched to reach out and touch the muscled planes of his chest. All in all, he looked much too tempting for her peace of mind.

He wrapped his fingers around her upper arm and tugged her through the doorway into the open-air corridor that looked out over the courtyard. "Thank you."

She turned so that she could see his profile in the moonlight. "You're welcome. Why didn't you come in?"

"I told you. Children need a woman's touch."

"Win, that's silly. Are you saying you don't think a father has a responsibility to comfort his children?" She whispered, not wanting to risk waking Shelly again.

Win's teeth flashed in the darkness as he smiled. "Don't get on your high horse, honey. I'm not saying that at all. It's just that right now, Shelly wants her mom. It makes sense that she'd accept more comfort from a woman."

"What about her dad?" Carlene asked, "Don't you think she misses him as well?"

Win snorted. "It wasn't her dad she was calling for."

Carlene had to acknowledge the truth in that statement. She shivered. The night chill reminded her that she'd forgotten to put on a robe, so did the expression in Win's eyes.

She tried valiantly to stay on topic. "That doesn't mean the children don't miss their dad."

He rubbed his hands up and down her arms, sending frissons of excitement through her as well as welcome warmth. "Mark travels a lot. They're used to him being gone for a few days at a time. This is the first time that Leah has left them with anyone for even overnight."

"Your sister must really be feeling pressed against a wall to have left them here."

"Yes." He pulled Carlene against him and wrapped his arms around her back. His heat enveloped her. "It's too cold out here for you wearing nothing but that thin gown."

She smiled at the censure in his voice and pulled back slightly so she could see his face. He looked dangerous in the reflected light of the moon.

"I was in too much of a hurry to find my robe. Besides, you're the one that pulled me out here instead of letting me return to my room and my warm bed. Why did you?"

"I wanted to talk to you."

"About Leah?"

His head lowered until his lips were centimeters from hers. "No."

Thoughts of Leah's emotional crisis faded as the flames of Win's desire reached out to lick her. She shivered again, but this time not from the cold. "Oh."

He smiled and lowered his mouth the remaining distance for their lips to touch.

* * *

Win waited a heartbeat, his lips pressed against Carlene's. Would she reject him? Desperation seized him as gaping hunger gnawed at his insides. He needed her softness so much, but he couldn't afford to push her tonight. He wanted her to agree to stay while Shelly and Jared were with him.

She gave a small, feminine moan and her lips softened under his. Exultation filled him as he deepened the kiss. He had been aching to taste and touch her since that one steamy encounter on his couch. Letting his hands slide down her back, he pressed her body more firmly against his. It felt so good.

Too good.

If he didn't sit down, he might well fall down. The acknowledgement of his weakness made him want to laugh. None of his men would believe that this tiny mite of a woman could bring him to his knees like this. Sweeping her into his arms, he carried her along to a wrought-iron lounger situated at the corner of the outdoor corridor. He liked to lie in it and watch the rain come down during a storm.

Without allowing their lips to break contact, he laid her on the cushion covering the lounger and came down on top of her.

She gasped as his body settled against hers.

Suddenly her fingers were all over him, touching his chest, his back, and finally burrowing into his hair as she pulled his face closer. She parted her lips and he eagerly accepted the invitation she offered. He swept her mouth with his tongue, reveling in the sounds of need emanating from her.

He wasn't sure, but he thought that her tiny little moans alone might be enough to make him spill his seed.

Still kissing her, he slipped to lie on the narrow width of cushion next to her. He kept one thigh locked over hers and pressed his erection against her hip, enjoying the sweet torture the position elicited. He wanted to touch her. He *needed* to touch her.

He undid the buttons on her prim cotton nightgown, pleased when she made no move to stop him. It was a far cry from the black lace he had been fantasizing her wearing, but the sight of her to-die-for body outlined by the thin cotton in the hall outside the kids' room had sent his temperature through the roof. It had also had an instant hardening effect on his sex.

Once her buttons were undone, he pulled back slightly and parted the soft white fabric to expose the perfection of her breasts. Strawberry-pink, velvet-soft nipples pointed proudly from the center of the creamy white mounds and it was all he could do not to bury his face between them.

He sucked in his breath. "You are incredible, honey. You know that? Looking at you is like being up close and personal to a piece of art."

The skin of her breasts flushed and he didn't think it was from arousal. "Win?"

"Hmm?" he asked as he slipped his hand inside and cupped one of her full breasts.

Damn. It felt as if he'd died and gone to heaven. Her nipple tightened under his palm and he couldn't resist brushing his hand back and forth, back and forth until she was pressing her generous flesh against the callused skin of his palms.

"I want to taste you."

Her head moved restlessly on the cushion. "Yes. Please. Win. *Yes*."

Pushing the fabric of her gown further to the side he lowered his head and closed his mouth over the puckered flesh.

She groaned and arched against his mouth. "Win, that feels… It's so… Please, don't stop."

He was happy to oblige. Hell, he was ecstatic. He suckled her sweet little nubbin while using his hand to gently squeeze and caress her other breast. He took her other nipple between his thumb and forefinger and pinched lightly. She cried out and arched against him, pressing his face into her breasts. Man, she was hot.

He could not wait to feel the slick warmth of her most private place. He wanted to touch it, to taste it, but most of all to bury himself in her until all that sweetness surrounded him and was branded with his touch.

He gripped her nightgown and started edging the fabric up until he could feel the bare skin on her leg. So soft. She was so incredibly soft. He inched his fingers up her thigh, seeking the tender flesh between her legs.

"Win? What are you doing?"

Did she really need him to explain it to her? He encountered the soft cotton of her panties. He rubbed her through the cotton, satisfied when it grew damp under his touch.

She gripped his shoulder, her fingernails digging into his skin. She would leave her mark on him and he didn't mind. Not at all.

"Win, please… This is too…"

He slipped one finger under the elastic of her panties and yes, right there. Yes. Wet. Hot. Slick feminine flesh.

"You can't touch me there," she shrieked.

He mentally disagreed even as he wondered at the panic in her voice. She acted like a nervous virgin.

Lifting his head, he tried to reassure her. "It's okay, honey. I like touching you there. I'll like it even more when we get your panties off. So will you."

Her eyes, which had been cloudy with passion, widened with something that looked like fear. "I don't want to take them off."

He begged to differ. "I think you want to, but you're scared. Tell me what's scaring you. I'll go slow. I swear."

"It's not that. It's just that I'm not sure I'm ready to make love with you, Win."

He felt irritation rising in him. "Why the hell not? You want me. You can't deny it."

He rubbed his finger over the feminine flesh hidden by her panties to prove his point. It worked too. She arched against his hand even as she shook her head.

"Don't shake your head at me, damn it. I won't let you lie to me. Not now. Not ever." He leaned over her, letting her see that he meant what he said.

She stared back at him, her eyes filled with some emotion he didn't understand. Finally, she nodded. "You're right. I *do* want you. Very much, but I *am* scared. Win, I don't want to be somebody's convenient bed partner for a short affair. Not even yours."

"I told you. I'm not looking for a sleazy affair," he ground out.

"Then what exactly are you looking for, Win? We both know it isn't a wife."

Helpless rage welled up in him. He wouldn't let another woman manipulate him into promising marriage in exchange for sex. He was a lot smarter at thirty than he had been at nineteen.

He jumped off the lounger and stood up, glaring down at her. "You're right. I don't want a wife, but I told you once before that there's a lot of ground between a one-night stand and marriage."

She stood and adjusted her nightgown so that her beautiful breasts and legs were back under cover. "Maybe there is for you, but I'm having a hard time accepting that."

Sexual frustration and anger made him lash out. "We both know that with a body like yours, you've had plenty of opportunity to figure it out. So, would you stop talking like a Victorian spinster, fearful of losing her virginity?"

She blanched as if he'd struck her. He felt about an inch tall and shrinking by the second as her eyes widened with pain and filled with tears.

Hell.

Before he had a chance to try to undo the damage he'd done with his mouth, she drew herself up and blinked away the moisture in her eyes.

"I'm getting awfully tired of explaining to the men around here that my bra size has no direct correlation to my desire to bed every male within a fifty-mile radius. I can understand Lonny's ridiculously immature view, but I expected more from you, Win. I really did."

She impatiently brushed an errant tear from her cheek. "Furthermore, I may not be Victorian, but I am a virgin and I can damn well talk like one if I want to."

With that she whirled and ran back down the corridor.

Win stood in stunned silence for a full thirty seconds, long enough for her to disappear inside her room. Then he swore a blue streak. Who would have guessed that a woman as good-looking as Carlene would be a virgin at twenty-six?

It wasn't natural.

He wanted to slam his fist into something.

* * *

The next morning, Win had already headed down to the stables by the time Carlene entered the kitchen.

She was a little late. She normally arrived for work at seven-thirty, but this morning she had dawdled getting dressed. She'd told herself that she had been busy listening for Shelly and Jared to wake, but the truth was that she was doing her level best to avoid Win.

She couldn't believe she'd done what she had with Win the night before…and enjoyed it so much. But he made her feel such intense things. Not only sexually, but different about herself—like her body was something truly beautiful. Something to be admired, not just lusted over. Which was pretty funny when lust and sex came together, but no way could she describe what happened last night as pure lust.

Win wanted her in a way that touched her so much more deeply than any man's interest had before because it felt deeper. He made her feel proud of her femininity…her figure.

But she still went hot with embarrassment every time she thought of the way she'd blurted out her virginity to him.

He must have had a good laugh at her expense after she fled like a frightened rabbit. Once he'd calmed his raging hormones, that was. The fear that he would accuse her of being a tease was another reason she was avoiding him. There was no denying that she'd encouraged him. And she'd been accused of being a tease by other men for a whole lot less.

Men like her ex-boss.

Shorty came into the kitchen. "Mornin', Carlene. Win says you'll need my help while the little 'uns are staying."

Carlene digested that. Win had made no such offer the day before and she knew he needed Shorty down in the stables, but she wasn't about to turn down the help, not when she had to cook for seven hungry men and keep two active toddlers occupied so they wouldn't miss their mom too much. "I could use a hand later getting lunch ready and started on dinner. It shouldn't take more than a couple of hours from your day."

"Good enough. Kitchen duty is a piece of cake compared to working with the boss today. He's ornery as a wounded mountain cat. I don't suppose you know anything about it, do you?"

She affected a nonchalance she didn't feel. "He's probably just a little stressed from worrying about his sister."

She opened the fridge and pulled out the meat she'd defrosted for tonight's dinner.

Shorty peered at her, his eyes intense. "I don't think so. He's used to dealing with Leah's troubles. Nope. It's something else and it's got him snapping at anyone fool enough to look cross-eyed. Thought for sure he was gonna take Lonny's head right off over something Win would have normally let go."

That got her attention. "He was mad at Lonny? Why?"

Shrugging, Shorty pulled out the big cast-iron stew pot and put it on the stove for her. "Can't rightly say. No real reason as far as I could see."

"Oh."

He turned and gave her another probing glance.

She forced a smile to her lips. "Why don't you go back to work? I won't need any help for a couple of hours."

Shorty shook his head. "Can't. Win said for me to watch the kiddies while you go to your apartment."

She stopped dicing the steak she planned to stew for shepherd's pie. "I wasn't planning to go to my apartment this morning."

"Win says you're going to need more things."

Win said this, Win said that. And just who said that Win was king and she one of his subjects?

When she didn't respond, Shorty added, "So you can stay the nights."

Carlene frowned at that. Win couldn't possibly know that she had changed her mind about staying. She hadn't said a thing. If anything, after last night, he should expect her to be even more entrenched in her certainty it was the wrong thing to do. She was a little surprised at herself that she wasn't. However, after holding Shelly while she cried the night before, Carlene knew she couldn't turn her back on Leah's children.

They did need her.

"I didn't tell Win I planned to stay the nights. In fact, I told him to find someone else."

"Kiddies need a woman's touch when they miss their mama."

Win and Shorty had hopelessly outdated views on the roles of gender in comfort. When she told Shorty she thought so, he shook his head, more serious than she'd ever seen him.

"Win spent a heap o' years being both parents to his little sister, long before his mama died in that plane crash. He's pretty determined to give Leah's kids what he couldn't give her, a woman to comfort them."

Sounds from the hall indicated the children had woken up. She moved to the sink to wash her hands. "I've got to feed the children right now. You might as well go back to work, Shorty."

She didn't admit that she planned to go to her apartment later. Win had no right to assume she meant to stay. The very least he could do was confirm it with her rather than sending Shorty to her with the news like a royal edict. She had valid reasons for not wanting to stay on Win's ranch and even if those reasons didn't weigh heavily against the feel of Shelly's little arms clinging around her neck, he didn't know she'd changed her mind. He was too arrogant for belief.

Shorty frowned, but didn't argue. It wouldn't have mattered if he had, she was already on her way to get the children up and dressed.

She decided that they could both use a bath after breakfast since she and Win hadn't bathed them the night before.

Two hours later, she was cutting fruit for a salad while Shelly and Jared played on the kitchen floor with the brightly colored plastic dishes Carlene used to store leftovers when Win entered the kitchen.

Both children shot up off the floor and wrapped themselves around Win's legs.

"Unca Win, I's a cook. See?" Jared stood proudly, covered from chest to toes in one of Carlene's white aprons that had been folded in half.

Win smiled down at his nephew and ruffled Jared's blond curls. "You making our dinner tonight, sport?"

Jared nodded. "In the *big* bowl. See?"

Win pretended to see an amazing array of dishes in the big bowl and commented on all of them. He gave Shelly a smacking kiss and told her to take Jared to see Shorty who would take them to visit the horses.

Shelly and Jared headed for Shorty, who was waiting by the outside kitchen door, with squeals of delight.

Win turned to Carlene, who had finished her salad and was sliding it onto an empty shelf in the refrigerator.

"Shorty and I'll keep an eye on the kids while you go to your apartment and pick up more spare clothes."

Not a word about last night. For which she should be grateful, but perversely wasn't.

She frowned at him. "I thought we agreed that you would find someone else to help you at night."

"Are you saying you're leaving?" Challenge radiated in his voice and stance, but she thought she saw fear in his eyes.

The fear decided her, but she wasn't going to make it easy for him. He could darn well have asked.

"We're not talking about me quitting my job. We're talking about me moving in here."

"Shelly and Jared need you. You saw that last night."

Sudden understanding dawned. "You waited, didn't you? You heard Shelly. Probably before I did, but you waited because you wanted me to go to her and to comfort her."

He had the grace to look guilty. "It was the hardest five minutes of my life. I hated hearing her cry," he admitted.

"And if I tell you it didn't work. That I still refuse to move in here until Leah comes back for her children?"

"Is that what you are saying?" he asked harshly.

He had told her last night never to lie to him. She didn't think she ever could.

She sighed. "No. That's not what I'm saying."

He nodded, the relief evident in his eyes, though she could see that he tried to hide it. He didn't sound relieved when he spoke however. He sounded irritated. "So, why the big scene about it?"

"You could have asked. Don't you realize how

arrogant you are to just assume I'll agree to stay, especially after last night?"

"So this is about last night? You want me to apologize? Fine. I'm sorry."

Unaccountable moisture burned the backs of her eyes. "I didn't ask for an apology."

He grabbed her arms and pulled her until their faces were inches apart. "Then what do you want?"

She closed her eyes against the anger in his and told him the truth. "I don't know anymore."

He let her go and she opened her eyes. He looked wary. "Are you ready to go to your apartment?"

She took a deep breath and nodded. "Yes. I'll be back after lunch. Everything is ready and in the refrigerator. Shorty will have to serve it, though."

"Fine." He turned to go back outside.

"Win."

He stopped at the door. "Yeah?"

"Do you have any idea how long Leah will be gone?"

He looked back over his shoulder, his expression closed. "No. Why?"

"It would be nice to know how much to pack and how long I'll be staying, but I guess that's out, huh?"

"I don't know. I wish I did."

The words were stark and suddenly it hit her that it bothered Win a whole lot more than it bothered her that he didn't know when his sister was coming back.

She tried to smile reassuringly at him. "It's going to be okay."

He nodded, but she could tell that he wasn't convinced.

"By the way, do you think she'd mind if I potty-trained Jared?"

His eyes widened. "I doubt it."

"Good."

"You sure you want to do it? I've heard potty-training can be pretty tough, especially for boys. I think that's why Leah's been putting it off."

She shrugged. "Trust me, a day and a half of changing a two-year-old's diapers is enough incentive for *me*."

She just wished she could find similar incentive to keep her hands and her thoughts off of her boss.

CHAPTER SIX

"YOU told me that Lonny asked you out and you turned him down."

Carlene looked up from the book she'd been trying to read.

His face set in an expression of disapproval, Win stood just inside her open bedroom door. She'd left it that way when she had put Shelly and Jared to bed. She wanted to be able to hear them if they needed her. Unfortunately, she had not heard Win's approach.

He had been busy down at the stables with a pregnant mare since after dinner and she hadn't expected to see him again until the following morning. She'd come to the conclusion late that afternoon that he was doing just as good a job of avoiding her as she had been doing to avoid him.

The knowledge had irritated her.

Especially after her trip to her apartment. She'd found herself packing lacy underwear and a couple of items of clothing that showed off her figure. She'd stopped in mid-packing, staring at a very pretty bra she hadn't worn since leaving Texas. It had been a symbol of her acceptance of herself then…something she'd lost when she left.

But she'd brought it with her to Win's house.

She shifted to sit up more squarely against the headboard and laid her book aside. "That's essentially what happened."

He ran his fingers through wet hair. He must have showered before hunting her down in her room. "I don't think so."

The dangerous emotion she sensed in him made her want to tread very carefully. "What do you mean?"

"Last night you said that he thought you wanted to go to bed with him."

She'd said several things she shouldn't have last night. "He offered. I turned him down. That's all there is to it."

"Lady, there's a hell of a difference between a man asking you to go out and offering to take you to bed." He pushed away from the doorway and stepped further into the room.

She felt as if the mountain cat Shorty had mentioned that morning had come in. She was tired of the feelings that overwhelmed her when Win was around. His interrogation over Lonny set off a recklessness she didn't understand, but she wasn't going to squelch either.

"Don't you think I know that? Don't you think

I've had enough experience with the latter my whole life to know that?"

He stopped prowling the room and fixed his blue-eyed gaze on her. "What do you mean?"

She slid her legs off the opposite side of the bed from where Win was standing and went to stand at the window. It looked out over the desert surrounding the ranch house. Moonlight reflected off the sagebrush and sparse Douglas Fir trees.

She started talking with her gaze still fixed on the night outside her window. "I started wearing a bra in the sixth grade and not some little-girl training bra either. Ever since then boys and then men assumed I was interested in sex."

"You telling me that some little ten-year-old tried to get you to drop your drawers behind the school building?"

She whipped around and glared at him. She was opening her heart to him; he could darn well take her seriously. "No. But, more than one not so little ten year old tried to get a feel of what was under my shirt."

She turned back to face the window, her face growing red with remembered shame. "It was humiliating. I was still playing with Barbies and boys thought I wanted to be their plaything. It just got worse as I got older. It wasn't just my breasts that developed. My whole body changed."

He spoke from right behind her, laying his hand on her shoulder. "Honey, you have a very nice body."

She almost laughed. "That was the whole problem. People assumed that I was a brainless twit because of the way I looked. By the time I hit high school, I lived in oversized clothes, kept my hair in an unstylish pony-tail and my nose buried in my books."

He turned her around to face him. "You're smart and you set out to prove that to everyone."

She nodded, surprised at his understanding. "Yes. I did it too. I graduated valedictorian with a full scholarship to a private university."

He tipped her chin up until their eyes met. "That's not the end of the story."

"How do you know?" she whispered the question.

"Because if it was you wouldn't still be so sensitive about a man's appreciation for your body."

That made her angry. "You think I should just laugh it off when men like Lonny try to cop a feel when no one else is around?"

Win's fingers on her shoulders went rigid. "He tried to cop a feel? You said he propositioned you."

"He did. He's obviously a believer in using multiple media to make a point."

"Hell."

His angry concern warmed her. "Look, Win. I handled it. Lonny won't be making any more passes."

He didn't look as if he believed her. "Like you handled it with me last night?"

"What do you mean? You think I let him kiss me and then called a halt to the whole thing? You think

I'm a tease?" She didn't care about Lonny any longer.
She just wanted to know if Win's avoiding her meant
that he thought she had led him on the night before
and was disgusted with her for it.

"No. That's not what I meant and you can stop
putting words into my mouth. I think you are a beautiful woman afraid of her own body, not a tease. You
were just as desperate to touch me as I was to touch
you, until you got scared. What I want to know is if
you thought you handled Lonny by telling him you
are a virgin. Because if you think that did it, I've got
bad news for you."

"What do you mean?" she asked, curious.

"He's more likely to see you as a challenge than
just let it go. He'll think that taking your virginity will
prove he's more of a man."

"Is that how you see me now, Win? A challenge?
Someone you need to bed to prove that you can do
what no other man has been able to accomplish?"
She had to know.

"We aren't talking about me. We're talking about
Lonny. Now tell me if you told him what you told
me," he demanded.

"No." she smiled wryly. "If you must know I used
multimedia as well."

"Explain," he demanded with typical Win-style ar-
rogance.

"I stomped on his foot to get him to back up and
when he did, I punched him."

His smile was slow and sexy. "You're some little Amazon when you're riled, aren't you, honey?"

She shrugged, secretly pleased at the approval she saw in his eyes. "When you grow up in west Texas, you learn how to take care of yourself. Now, answer my question. Am I just a challenge to you?"

His smile faded and his eyes became very intense. "Carlene, I need you like I haven't needed a woman in a long time, maybe ever. It hasn't got a damn thing to do with your lack of experience. In fact, I spent most of last night trying to convince myself to leave you the hell alone."

She looked around her room and then back at Win. "But you didn't succeed."

"No."

"I still don't want an affair."

"I'm still not interested in marriage." He released her and swung away. He walked over to her bed and picked up the book she had been reading.

It was a romantic suspense by her favorite author. She should have known she was in trouble when she'd been unable to concentrate on it.

He laid the book back down and turned around to face her again. The expression on his face chilled her. "My ex-wife used sex to manipulate me into marriage, Carlene. I won't let that happen again."

The knowledge that he'd been married before hurt her. "Where does that leave us, Win?"

"I don't know. Are you going to use my attraction to you to try to force marriage?"

A painful lump formed in her throat. "No, but I'm not going to have a casual affair with you either."

His hands clenched at his sides. "I guess there's nothing left to say, then, is there?"

He turned and headed toward the door. With each step he took, she wanted to stop him, to call him back. But for what?

She didn't have an answer to the impasse they found themselves in either.

Three days later, Carlene was exhausted and cranky as she shucked the corn on the cob she planned to serve Win and the hands for dinner that night. Grateful that she had a smaller number to feed than usual, she yanked the husk off the outside of the corn and tossed it in the bag at her feet. A couple of the ranch hands were delivering a stud Win had sold to another Mustang breeder in Wyoming. They weren't expected back until tomorrow.

She kept an eye on Shelly and Jared out of the corner of her eye. They were playing in a small plastic pool that Win had purchased for them. She'd wanted to set it up in the courtyard, but they wanted to watch the horses and she'd compromised, setting the pool up outside the back entrance to the kitchen, telling the kids they'd have to watch the horses from that distance. Jared splashed Shelly and the little girl gave a gleeful shout.

Carlene smiled despite her irritable mood. Win had been right when he said they were "a couple of real cute kids". Watching them had confirmed her own desire to be a mother. Something she wasn't likely to become anytime soon.

"Miss Carlene, Miss Carlene. Jared has to go potty. Can I take him?" asked Shelly while Jared hopped on one foot, looking desperate.

Shelly loved escorting her brother to the bathroom and setting up the potty chair for him. It made her feel like a big girl, so Carlene agreed.

She'd just finish shucking the corn and then go make sure Jared got his big-boy underwear pulled up right.

She brushed the back of her hand against the slight perspiration on her forehead. She needed a nap. Between Shelly waking up in the middle of the night and thoughts of Win that disturbed Carlene's rest, she had been getting precious little sleep the past few days.

Shelly hadn't woken the night before last. She seemed to be settling into the routine of the ranch, but then Leah had called last night and spoken to the children. It had been almost impossible to get Shelly and Jared to sleep and then, predictably, Shelly had woken around midnight calling for her mother.

Carlene had rocked the little girl for over an hour before Shelly had fallen back asleep.

Win told Carlene that Leah had said she just

needed a few more days and then she'd be back. He
hadn't volunteered anything else and Carlene hadn't
asked. Truthfully, she didn't care when Leah got back
except how it affected Shelly and Jared.

Carlene's main concern was the fear that she was
falling in love with her boss, a man who would
probably never let himself love her. He'd been very
careful to avoid any physical contact with her for
the last three days and it was driving her crazy.
When their hands accidentally collided while
bathing the children, he would yank his away as if
she burned him.

His constant rejection made her want to cry, but
not half so much as the haunted expression she saw
on his face whenever he really looked at her.

Win still wanted her, of that she was certain. But
how long would he want her? He wasn't looking for
a lifetime commitment and Carlene wasn't foolish
enough to believe that a temporary physical attraction would lead to anything more than heartache for
her. She hated the fact that Win equated her desire
for a strong commitment to manipulation. It wasn't
that she wanted to force him to marry her.

What she needed was the security that they were
both going into the relationship wanting to make it last,
looking at the possibility of a future together. She
couldn't have a future with a man who refused to
marry, could she?

The knowledge that he'd been married once

before gnawed at her. He had loved one woman enough to risk the commitment despite his experience growing up with a mother who changed husbands as often as some women changed hairstyles. What had ended his first marriage? Did he still love his ex-wife?

That question tormented Carlene more than any other. The thought of Win loving another woman made her want to throw up.

She finished shucking the corn and stood up. Time to check on the kids. She was surprised that they hadn't come back outside to continue playing in the pool. When she tried to open the kitchen door, though, she found it locked. Panic pulsed through her until she heard giggles from the inside.

The children weren't hurt.

She rushed around to the kitchen window and, standing on her tip-toes, tried to peer inside. She wasn't tall enough. She looked around her for something to stand on; her gaze fell on a wooden crate one of the hands had left near the house. She dragged it over to the window and stepped up, this time getting a clear view of the kitchen.

The sight that met her eyes made her sigh with relief and groan in exasperation. Jared stood in the center of the floor wearing one of Carlene's large white aprons and holding a wooden spoon. Shelly stood on a chair with a box of cereal. She poured the cereal onto the floor into a large puddle of milk as

Carlene watched helplessly through the window. Jared stirred it with the spoon.

"Something wrong, Carlene?"

Win's voice startled her and she lost her balance. Her arms windmilled and the bag of corn she had been holding went flying just before she did. Win caught her, but several small thuds indicated the corn hadn't been so lucky.

Landing against Win's chest, she expelled air in a big whoosh. For a brief moment in time, she forgot the children making cereal on the floor she'd mopped just that morning. She forgot her fears for the future. She forgot that Win had been avoiding her. All she could think about was the feel of Win's strong arms locked around her and his rock-hard body pressed against her own.

It didn't matter that he only held her because she'd literally flown through the air to land in his arms. He was holding her and it felt good, too good. Her eyes wide, she licked her lips, trying to find something to say.

He swore and then lowered his mouth to hers.

The kiss was brief, but explosive. Although he pulled back almost immediately, she had felt the desperate hunger in him and it called to a matching emotion in her.

He set her away from him. "I didn't mean to do that."

"I know."

She did too. He'd made it abundantly clear that he didn't want to start anything under her terms. She forced herself to look away from him and noticed the corn strewn on the ground. She wanted to scream out her frustration, but swallowed the urge. She bent down and started to gather the corn.

"Just rinse it and it'll be fine," Win said as he picked up the corn near him and tossed it into her bag.

She raised her head and glared at him. "Easy for you to say. You're not responsible for feeding the hands. I am."

Win's eyes narrowed. "Take it easy, honey. No one's going to notice that the corn took a detour on the way to the table."

"Maybe not, but they're bound to notice when they have to eat it raw because Shelly and Jared locked the cook out of the kitchen."

Win's smile infuriated her. It wasn't funny, darn it. "Don't you dare laugh. This is not in the least amusing."

He tried to hide his smile. "No. I can see that."

"Just what do you think Leah would say if she drove up right now? She wouldn't be very impressed that the woman you hired to watch her children had managed to get herself locked out of the house while they had a merry old time making cereal on the floor."

"Is that what they're doing? Making cereal?" he asked.

"Yes, with an entire box of toasted oats and about a gallon of milk from the looks of things." Just the thought of all that milk spilled on her newly mopped floor made her wince.

Win turned toward the house. "Come on."

She followed him to the kitchen door. Win pounded on the door. "Shelly, open up. Miss Carlene and I want to come inside."

Carlene heard movement from within and then the door scraped open. Shelly stood on the other side, her face split in a happy grin. "Hi. Me and Jared got hungry. We made cereal."

Carlene's gaze settled on the little boy sitting in the middle of the floor, eating the soggy cereal with his fingers. He looked up and smiled proudly. "I's a cook. See?"

Part of her wanted to laugh and the other part wanted to make sure the children knew that locking her out of the kitchen and making cereal on the floor was not appropriate behavior.

She settled on turning to glare at Win, who had swung Shelly up into his arms. "Do you still think this is humorous?"

Win indicated his nephew with a flick of his eyes. "Yep. You can't tell me that's not funny, Carlene."

She sighed. So much for help from that quarter. She walked over to Jared and lifted him from the puddle of cereal. "Come on, sweetie, let's get you cleaned up."

Jared protested, "But I's a cook. Don't wanna get cleaned."

"You're a good cook too, Jared. As a matter of fact, I'm going to let you and Shelly help me make dinner, but first we've got to wash you up. Cooks have to be very clean when they're making food for other people."

"Oh."

She took that for agreement and headed toward the bathroom.

She looked at Win over her shoulder. "You can bring Shelly. I'll need your help getting them both bathed before I clean up the mess in the kitchen."

Win's eyes narrowed. "I've got stuff to do in the stable. I don't have time to give the kids a bath right now."

Carlene gave him her sweetest, most insincere, smile. "Just think of it as an *amusing* blip in your schedule."

Win growled something that made Shelly laugh.

By the time she and Win had Jared and Shelly bathed and changed, both children were showing signs that they needed a nap. Carlene got them to lie down with the promise that she would wait to finish preparing dinner until they woke up.

Win followed her back into the kitchen. "Need help cleaning up this mess?" he asked, indicating the cereal drying to the floor.

"I thought you had things to do."

"They'll keep."

She shook her head. "That's okay. Cleaning it up is my penance for letting this happen in the first place."

"How did you?"

She wasn't about to admit that she'd gotten side-tracked thinking about him.

She shrugged. "I guess I'm a little tired. I let Shelly take Jared to the bathroom and I didn't keep very close track of the time that had passed. The next thing I knew, they had locked me out and were pouring milk on my newly mopped floor."

Win's eyes filled with concern. "You aren't getting enough sleep."

"It was just sitting out in the sunshine being lazy. It made me tired. I'm fine now." A yawn surprised her before she could stifle it, giving lie to her words.

He reached out and brushed her cheek. "You've got shadows under your eyes. I should have noticed. You're working too hard."

"I'm fine, really." She didn't think her heart could handle his concern. She'd rather he went back to ignoring her.

He shook his head. "You need a nap as much as the kids do. Go lie down and I'll take care of cleaning up this mess."

A nap sounded so tempting, but cleaning was her job after all. "Don't be silly. You didn't hire me so you'd have to clean up when I'm feeling a little sleepy."

"Forget the mess," he growled. "You're taking a nap."

She would have argued, but another yawn slipped out and she knew Win would never believe that she didn't need the rest. She nodded. "Fine, but don't complain to me about getting behind on your own work."

He nudged her toward the door. "You're welcome."

She didn't need to be such a fishwife. Turning around, she gave him a conciliatory smile. "I'm sorry, Win. Thank you. Though I'm sure Lonny and Shorty won't be thanking me for keeping you from the stables."

She turned to go, but his words stopped her. "Lonny isn't with Shorty."

Her tired brain had a difficult time making sense of his statement, but she sensed there was something important there that she needed to understand.

She turned around to face him again. "Where is he, then?"

Win's shoulder's lifted in a negligent gesture that said he didn't know. "I fired him."

"You fired him? Why?" She couldn't believe it.

Win looked at her as if her brain wasn't functioning very well, which it wasn't. However, her question was a reasonable one.

"He made a pass at you," Win said.

"But, I took care of it. You didn't have to fire him."

A frown creased Win's features. "He signed his own pink slip the moment he touched you."

She couldn't take it in. "That's ridiculous, Win. This is your busiest time of year. You can't have fired one of your hands just because he made a play for your housekeeper."

Suddenly he was right in front of her, his hands holding her in place. "You aren't just my house-keeper, damn it."

"Yes, I am. You're interested in sleeping with me like Lonny was, but I'm no more than your employee."

His expression turned fierce. "I'm not like Lonny and you know it."

Weary of fighting over the same ground, she conceded. "You're right. You are old enough to go out with me for one thing, but you want the same thing he did."

Win released her and let his arms drop to his side. "Lonny's a horny kid on the prowl for a good lay. I want *you*, honey. There's a difference and one of these days you're going to figure it out. Then you'll put us both out of our misery."

She opened her mouth to deny what he had said, but he pressed one of his fingers against her lips. "Shh. Go take your nap. We'll talk about this later."

She swallowed her denial and, pulling away from him, she turned to go.

Win finished cleaning the kitchen, careful to get every last bit of milk mopped up. Carlene wouldn't appreciate the smell of sour milk in her kitchen. He liked the possessiveness with which she referred to the kitchen. Other housekeeper-cooks had said similar things, but hearing it had never affected Win the same way. It made him feel a sense of permanence with Carlene; like maybe she wouldn't quit and move on the way she'd told him she planned to do eventually.

He rinsed the mop with bleach water and put it away in the broom closet. Then, although he knew he needed to get to the stable, he found himself climbing the stairs to the second level and walking down the corridor toward Carlene's room. He took a minute to check on Jared and Shelly. Both kids were sleeping soundly, which didn't surprise Win at all. They expended enough energy to fuel a small town. He didn't know how Carlene handled it. Even with Shorty's help in the afternoons, she must be running herself ragged, but she hadn't contacted a service to send someone out to help her.

When he had asked her why, she shrugged and said she didn't think the kids needed another stranger in their life right now.

She was an amazing woman.

He pushed open her bedroom door and his gaze settled on the woman sleeping in the bed. She'd undressed and her bare shoulder peaked above the light blanket she slept under. His fingers itched to touch the silky smooth skin. How long was she going to keep him waiting? When would she accept that they could be good together?

Good, nothing. They would be spectacular.

She sighed in her sleep and turned her head on the pillow, giving him an unencumbered view of her gentle features. Bruises from lack of sleep marked the skin under her eyes. He felt guilt settle on him. Hell. He should have noticed how tired she was getting, but he'd been so busy trying to avoid her. He'd spent the last three days trying to give her space.

He realized now that the strategy hadn't worked worth a hill of beans.

She was still focused on his desire to remain single. She couldn't seem to grasp the fact that he wanted more than some tawdry affair or a one-night stand. He almost laughed. One night with Carlene would only leave him hungry for more. As he'd told her, there was a whole range of possibilities between marriage and a quick roll in the hay.

Wasn't there?

Of course there was, he admonished himself.

She didn't think so.

Hell. She'd even compared him to that idiot, Lonny. It was not a flattering comparison. Lonny would bed any willing woman. Win should have realized the potential for trouble when he hired Carlene. He hadn't. The knowledge rankled.

She should never have found herself in the position of having to defend her virtue from a lecher like Lonny.

Well, Win would be much more careful when he hired a replacement hand. He wouldn't hire another jerk looking for an easy lay, even if it meant working the busy spring season short one stable hand. He would protect Carlene, even if she didn't think she needed it.

CHAPTER SEVEN

"Anybody up for some ice cream?" Win asked after dinner.

His question was immediately greeted with delighted shouts by his niece and nephew.

"I wants some. I do," shouted Jared.

"Me too. I want bubble gum flavor. Can I have bubble gum, Uncle Win?" Shelly asked, hopping excitedly from one foot to the other in the middle of the kitchen.

Win turned to Carlene and she felt the force of his gaze as it locked with hers over the children's heads. "How about you, Carlene? Would you like something sweet and cool?"

She wanted *something,* but ice cream didn't come into it. Ever since she'd woken from her nap, she'd been feeling a curious tension. It felt as if something had shifted in her relationship with Win that afternoon, but she didn't yet understand what.

Perhaps it had something to do with his remark

about putting them both out of their misery. About wanting her, not just any woman. She had the distinct impression that a showdown over their relationship was coming, one in which she might not be victorious. She wasn't even sure she wanted to be any longer. Ice cream, however, was safe.

So she nodded. "Sure, just let me do something to my hair and I'll be ready to go."

Gazing at her reflection in the vanity mirror in the bathroom attached to her room a few minutes later, she critically surveyed the dark curls framing her makeup-free face. She hadn't had time to apply any sort of cosmetics since the first morning after she started watching Win's niece and nephew. Children were time-consuming. No wonder so many mothers went for the natural look.

Grimacing at the unkempt woman in the mirror, she made a decision. Twenty minutes later, she had changed her clothes, swept her hair up in a riot of curls on top of her head and applied subtle makeup. She moved into the bedroom and took inventory of her improved appearance. She looked much more feminine in the form-fitting, coral knit top, emerald-green designer jeans and gold sandals than she had in her oversized white T-shirt, blue jeans and tennis shoes she'd been wearing earlier.

Win called impatiently from the courtyard. She could hear the children playing in the fountain through the opening she had left cracked in her door.

"Carlene, by the time you're ready it's going to be winter already and ice cream isn't going to sound so good."

She smiled at the jibe, anticipating Win's reaction to the change from frumpy housekeeper to attractive female. Taking the time to apply coral lip-gloss over the too-subtle lipstick she had originally picked out, Carlene finished getting ready. She seized her purse off the dresser and headed to the courtyard to meet Win and the children.

The minute she stepped onto the stone pathway, she knew her time primping had been well spent.

Win's eyes locked on her with the precision of a homing missile. A slow, wicked grin split his face. "Honey, it's a good thing for you that we've got these two around or you'd never make it to town for ice cream."

His hand swept out, indicating the children, who were sailing two small plastic vessels in the pool below the fountain.

She returned his smile with one of her own and winked. "Maybe I wouldn't want to."

The intensity in his look shot up another ten degrees. He took a deep breath. "You're playing with fire, honey. Watch it or you're going to end up singed."

"Uncle Win, Mama says never to play with fire. It's dangerous." Shelly's sweet face was set in serious lines.

Win laughed and the sound of masculine amusement shivered along Carlene's nerve endings with as much force as a touch.

He swept Shelly up in his arms and tickled her. "You're right, sweetpea. Fire is dangerous."

Turning his head, he met Carlene's gaze and she knew the words were meant for her as much as for his niece.

Feeling too good to be cautious, Carlene just smiled and turned to collect Jared.

That nap had done wonders.

Several other families shared Win's brilliant plans for after-dinner ice cream. The place was packed.

Families. The word didn't really describe himself, Carlene and the children. Technically, he, Shelly and Jared could be considered family, but it wasn't the same. He didn't plan on getting married again and that meant he wasn't going to be a father. It also meant he didn't have to worry about disappointing his children as his parents had disappointed him. It meant he wouldn't bring another child into the world that would have to face the devastation of divorce and his *family* getting ripped apart.

It also meant that Win would never have a wife or children to share the simple pleasures in life, like going out for ice cream on a warm summer evening.

Thoughts that used to underline his hard-won independence were now just a little depressing. He gave himself a mental shake and focused on the pleasure of the moment. He was with his two favorite kids and a warm, sexy woman. What more could a man ask for?

Answers that he didn't want to deal with whispered at the back of his mind, but he ignored them in favor of glaring at a couple of teenage boys that were ogling Carlene. One of the boys caught his gaze and quickly turned away, nudging his friend as he did so. The friend wasn't so quick to look away, but when Win indicated the outside with a tilt to his head and a raised eyebrow, the boy swallowed and found a renewed interest in the menu board.

He'd never felt this possessive about anyone, not even his ex-wife. Rachel had been pretty. Men had looked and all Win had experienced had been male satisfaction in having a pretty wife. Carlene would probably call him sexist. Hell, maybe he was...a little. Anyway, things were different with Carlene and they weren't even involved yet.

"What are you going to have?" Her question pulled Win from his reverie.

He shrugged. "Double scoop of Rocky Road. It's what I always have."

She stared at him as if he'd just said that he ate his ice cream while riding buck naked through town.

"What?" he demanded. "You don't like Rocky Road?"

"I love Rocky Road, but I can't imagine getting

the same flavor of ice cream every single time. They've got thirty-two flavors, Win. How can you not want to try something new? I can't even get two scoops of the same thing," she admitted.

"I'm not much on change I guess."

"Life without change is boring. It's too…it's too…*predictable*."

Yeah. Like waking up next to the same husband for the rest of your life. His mom hadn't liked that sort of predictability either. "That's me, boring."

Making a grab for Jared's shirt before he could get out the door someone had just opened, Carlene laughed. She led Jared over to the case that displayed ice-cream cones decorated like clowns and animals. "Here, sugarbear. Why don't you pick one of these to have for your treat?"

Shelly decided she wanted a decorated cone as well and joined Jared at the case as they discussed the merits of the ones displayed there.

Carlene turned back to Win, lingering laughter in her eyes. "One thing you could never be, Win, is boring. Irritating. Arrogant and sometimes even predictable, but never boring."

"Tell me that six months from now." That was about how long his mom's euphoria over a new marriage would last. Then the fighting would start. The tantrums came next and then, finally, divorce.

Carlene's smile slipped. "I get the feeling we're talking about more than preferences in ice cream here."

He shrugged. A crowded restaurant was not the place to get into such a discussion. In fact, he didn't think he wanted to have this particular discussion at all. "What two different flavors are you going to have this time?"

She eyed him speculatively, as if she was testing his determination to change the subject, and then she too shrugged. "I was thinking about the flavor of the month and mocha almond fudge. I'll have it as a sundae with hot fudge, whip cream, nuts and a cherry, of course."

It was his turn to eye her askance. "What is the point of ordering two different flavors if you're going to drown them with toppings?"

The sparkle came back to her eyes. Laying her hand against his chest, she said, "You've definitely got to learn to live a little, Win. Your ice-cream-eating education has been severely limited. I suggest you let me order for you tonight."

He couldn't resist the teasing glint in her eyes. She'd been like this ever since she came into the courtyard looking like a million bucks. He liked it when she teased him, he realized. Taking the plunge, he said, "Okay."

Her smile went up about one hundred watts. "Great."

For a minute he thought she was going to seal her approval with a kiss. She had slipped her hand up from his chest to the back of his neck and her gaze had gone soft, her lips parting. He started to lean down to make it easy for her and she blinked. Then she looked around, seeming to remember their surroundings.

Lightning quick, she removed her hand from his neck and moved back a step. "Uh, I'll find out which cones Shelly and Jared have decided on."

Stifling his disappointment, he nodded. "You do that."

His voice came out harsher than he intended. He knew she wanted to be discreet, but he didn't have to like it.

She didn't waste any time moving further away from him toward the kids.

"I want the puppy," Shelly said in response to Carlene's question.

Jared wanted a lime-green clown.

Win took the kids to a table to sit down while Carlene made the order. He wondered what kind of ice cream he was going to end up having. He doubted it would matter. Ten to one, she was going to have it all doctored up like hers.

A few minutes later when she appeared at their table with two fully loaded sundaes and the kids' cones, his guess was confirmed. Carlene laid a huge stack of napkins in the middle of the table along with a cup of water. She handed each of the kids their cones before placing what looked like a mound of whip cream in front of Win. He speculated on what the innocent-looking white fluff hid before scooping into it with his spoon.

His trepidation must have shown on his face because she giggled. "Don't worry, it isn't going to bite back."

"That's what they said before the giant banana split destroyed that small Midwestern town."

Shelly's eyes rounded. "What giant 'nana split? Did you see it?"

He reached out and ruffled his niece's hair. "No, sweetpea. I was just kidding."

"Oh. Does that mean the giant 'nana split isn't true, Uncle Win?"

He nodded. "Yes, sweetpea, that's what it means."

"Mama says you aren't supposed to lie, Uncle Win."

He groaned and looked to Carlene for help. Her gaze was fixed on someone behind him and he got the feeling she'd missed most of the frustrating exchange he was having with Shelly.

He wanted to turn and see who she was looking at with that expression of chagrin, but he had to answer Shelly's question first. He didn't want her telling Leah that he lied.

"A joke isn't a lie, sweetpea, because nobody is supposed to believe it. They're supposed to think it's funny."

"When somethin's funny I laugh," Shelly informed him.

"It was a joke for Carlene," he said, feeling just a little irritated at both the constant questions and Carlene's fixation with whoever had just walked in.

"Miss Carlene didn't laugh." Shelly's observation didn't improve Win's mood any.

He fixed Carlene with an irritated frown. "No, she didn't."

Shelly turned her attention to Carlene as well. "Miss Carlene, why didn't you laugh?"

Carlene turned to Shelly, making an obvious effort to collect her thoughts. "What was I supposed to laugh at?"

Shelly gave an exaggerated sigh. "Uncle Win's joke, silly. He said it was funny, but you didn't laugh."

Carlene shifted her gaze to Win. He stared back, letting her see his irritation. She let out her own little sigh. "I'm sorry, Win. I missed it. Do you want to repeat it?"

He wanted to know what had her so rattled. "No. Humor lacks something when the spontaneity is missing."

She winced. "Sorry. Uh, what do you think of your sundae?"

He looked down at the melting whip cream covering a mound of ice cream and toppings he had barely touched. "What is it?"

"French vanilla with hot fudge." She reached over and dipped one of the napkins in the cup of water. Then, using the wetted napkin, she wiped the dripping ice cream from Jared's fingers before handing him back his cone.

Then she turned her attention to Win. She

reached across the table and picked up his spoon. After scooping a bite of the concoction in his bowl onto it, she offered it to him. "Here, scaredy-cat. Take a bite."

He would have told her he wasn't afraid to try it, but when he opened his mouth she slid the spoon inside, managing to make it feel like a caress in his mouth. He licked the ice cream off the pink plastic spoon and she slowly withdrew it from his mouth. Then, spying a smidgen of fudge left on the plastic, she put it in her own mouth and licked it off.

"It's one of my favorites. Do you like it?"

The sundae was delicious, but the sight of Carlene licking the spoon was sweet enough to give him a sugar rush. He took another bite of ice cream and swirled it around in his mouth pretending to think about it.

Carlene waited with anxious anticipation on her face for his verdict. He took another bite, making this one last longer than the last one. She seemed mesmerized by the way he ate his ice cream.

"It's fine."

Her eyes narrowed, but she couldn't hide her small, shallow breaths. "Fine? I order you the classic of all classics in ice cream confectionery and you say it's just fine?"

He kept his expression neutral. "It's not quite the same experience as a double-scoop cone of Rocky Road."

She sized him up with her gaze. "I see. I guess

next time I'll let you order your own ice cream. Some people just don't adjust well to change."

He laughed. "Honey, it's ambrosia and you know it." Did she know how much he'd enjoyed her feeding him as well?

She must have because every once in a while she'd offer him a bite of her ice cream, or dip her spoon in his and feed it to him. The kids wanted to get in on the act, so Carlene shared hers with them, too. How she managed to be sweet and motherly with his niece and nephew and in almost the same breath turn around and send his hormones raging, he didn't know. But, man, he liked. He liked it a lot.

They were finishing their ice cream when he heard his name.

"Win Garrison. That you?"

He turned and looked up. Grant Strickland was striding toward them. Win stood and shook hands with the other man. "Strickland. How's married life treating you?"

Grant's new wife, Zoe, had been one of Leah's friends when they were younger. Win hadn't gone to the wedding because he actually didn't know Grant and Zoe all that well. Leah was the one that had actually done part of her growing up and schooling here in Sunshine Springs. He and his sister had moved into Hank Garrison's ranch home with their mother when Win was seventeen. Grant had been in his class in high school, but Win had been too busy learning the ropes of ranch life from Hank after school to make many friends.

Besides, Win made it a policy to avoid weddings whenever possible.

Grant's smile was so blissful it was almost painful. "I'm a happy man."

Win believed him. Maybe marrying your best friend was the one way a man could figure she wasn't going to grow bored and leave. If she wanted to marry you after knowing you most of her life, she wasn't likely to change her mind six months down the road.

Grant focused his gaze over Win's shoulder. "Hey, Carlene."

"Hi, Grant." Her voice was quiet.

"You two know each other?" Win asked.

"I met him at the Dry Gulch."

Win nodded. "She's working for me now, as my housekeeper."

Grant's eyes widened in surprise, but his attention didn't linger on Carlene. Leaning down, he ruffled Jared's hair. "Hi, little guy. Leah's your momma, isn't she?"

Jared just ducked his head, but Win nodded. "Yep, these are Leah's little ones."

"I didn't realize that Leah was in town. Zoe'll want to see her."

Carlene's smile slipped and Win wondered if she was worried about him telling Grant that she was living at Win's ranch temporarily while Leah's kids were staying.

Win shrugged. "Actually, she's not in town. Leah left the kids with me for a few days."

Grant didn't ask any questions as a woman would have. He just nodded. "I don't know if you've heard, but I've decided to shift the focus of my ranch from cattle to horses."

"I heard."

Leah had told him that Zoe, a vegetarian, got too upset when the cattle went to the stock sale. Grant was changing his ranch and the way he made his livelihood to make his wife happy. Win wondered if he'd be willing to do the same thing for Carlene. The thought was so alien it made him frown. He had no plans to marry, not Carlene. Not anyone. She affected him as no other woman had, but he was still in control of his future and that future did not include a wedding.

"I was hoping you'd let me pick your brain on the running of a horse ranch. I'm not going to try to run a stable as well like you have, but I'm real interested in the Mustang herd. You've got one of the best reputations in the business."

Win nodded, not at all flustered by the praise. It was true and he'd worked damn hard to make it that way. No sense denying it. "Come out anytime. I'll show you around the operation although the ranch is pretty much Joe's baby now. I'm damn busy with the stables."

Grant laughed. "That's what happens when you're the best at what you do."

"Or at least in the top ten," Win said with a smile.

Grant nodded. "Well, Zoe's at the pizza place. I saw your truck outside and decided to come in. I'd better not keep her waiting."

Grant turned to go, waiving a quick farewell over his shoulder to Carlene and Leah's children.

When Win turned around, Carlene was busy washing Shelly's face and hands. Jared looked as if he could use a little help too. Win dipped another napkin in the water and went to work on his nephew.

When he was finished, he asked Carlene, "You ready to go?"

"Sure. We'd better get these two in bed soon." She didn't quite meet his eyes and he wondered what she was thinking.

Was she regretting her earlier teasing? Did she think he would make her follow through on the offer she'd made in the courtyard before they left? The kids would be in bed soon, but he didn't know what that was going to buy him.

Sometimes the female mind was too complicated for a mere man to comprehend.

Carlene tucked the blankets around Shelly and prayed that the little girl would sleep through the night.

Leaning down to kiss the soft skin of Shelly's cheek, Carlene said, "Goodnight, sweet girl."

Shelly smiled sleepily. "Goodnight, Miss Carlene."

Her eyes were closed before Carlene had turned to take Jared from Win's arms. Win had changed the boy into pajamas and night-time underwear in case of accidents. Win shook his head at Carlene. "I'll tuck him in."

She nodded and left the room. She hadn't expected Win to give her such an easy escape after her earlier teasing, but she certainly wasn't going to make things more difficult for herself by sticking around.

The rumble of Win's voice as he spoke to Jared trickled down the hall as Carlene made her way to her bedroom. She turned on the light and shut the door, relief flowing over her that she was saved from the confrontation over their relationship—at least for tonight.

What had possessed her to tease Win as she had in the courtyard, and then later at the ice cream shop? She had been playing with fire and Win was right. If she didn't watch it, she was going to end up good and burned. Kicking off her sandals, she headed to the bathroom to wash off her makeup and brush her teeth.

Seeing Grant tonight had been a shock. She should have expected it. After all, he and Zoe lived on a ranch on the other side of Sunshine Springs. Carlene was bound to run into them once in a while. It wasn't as if there were hard feelings between them either. She'd been invited to their wedding…and she'd gone. But seeing Grant while she was with Win had been disconcerting.

It made her realize how much of a mistake she'd made with him.

Unclipping her hair, she let it fall to her shoulders in a springy mass of dark curls. She finger-combed it, knowing the tight natural curls would just frizz out if she attempted to brush her hair out now that it was dry.

She had tried straightening it once. Her mother had thought that doing so might give her a more staid appearance, a more *acceptable* appearance. Carlene had found the procedure and the results less than pleasant. As she finished detangling her hair with her fingers she realized that her mother might never accept her as she was. She looked in the mirror and conceded that after her parent's refusal to stand by her during the problems she had faced back home, that was no longer as important as it once had been.

However, that didn't mean she couldn't accept herself. Life was too complicated as it was without trying to be someone else.

So, who was she?

Was she the woman who had dressed in spandex miniskirts and tended bar at the Dry Gulch or was she the woman who wore her clothes loose and comfortable while tending house and cooking for Win Garrison?

She moved back into her bedroom and took a fleeting glance at the woman in the mirror. Perhaps she wasn't either of those women. Perhaps she was the woman standing before her, looking back from the mirror. A woman comfortable enough with her own body that she could wear clothes that enhanced her figure without needing to flamboyantly display every curve.

One thing was certain, she wasn't the woman who had donned her work gear and tried to seduce Grant Strickland. Her face heated at the memory. Grant had asked her out first. The date had ended in disaster when Zoe's pet hamster had come running into the kitchen.

Carlene had an unreasonable fear of rodents.

The second date, if you could call it that, had been entirely her idea. Grant had stopped by the Dry Gulch with a dozen red roses and Carlene had assumed that meant he was interested in pursuing a relationship.

Looking back, she couldn't understand what had prompted her to act like a siren. The only explanation that she could think of was that for a month or two before Grant asked her out, she had become increasingly depressed and lonely, not to mention restless with her innocent and single status.

Grant was the first man that she had any real interest in for so long that she went for it. She acted out the part she assumed he had been expecting when he asked her out, that of the seductress. She didn't seduce him. She succeeded in humiliating herself and causing a rift between Grant and Zoe. In her own defense, she had not realized that the two had become a couple. They'd been friends so long, no one, including Carlene, thought they ever would.

She didn't think that mid-life crises occurred at twenty-six, but she didn't have a better explanation for her behavior. It certainly bore no resemblance to her refusal to sleep with Win. It wasn't as if she had asked Grant if he were interested in marriage either. So, why make such a big deal out of it with Win? Why refuse herself and Win the sensual relief they both craved because of their lack of a future? It wasn't as if she'd been sure she could have a future with Grant Strickland.

In a moment of stunning clarity she realized that although she had been attracted to Grant, she had been in no danger of falling in love with him. Their lack of a future hadn't bothered her because she hadn't necessarily wanted one with him, but she did with Win. She knew instinctively that if she gave herself to Win, she would be opening herself up to heartache beyond anything she had ever experienced—even the rejection of her parents.

She plopped down onto the side of the bed, unable to accept what her heart was trying to tell her. She could not allow herself to love a man who believed the solution to life's problems lay in a no strings attached, short term affair. She couldn't.

The only problem was that she had a horrible feeling that she already had.

She was so overwhelmed by her thoughts that she

only vaguely registered the knock on her door. It wasn't until the door swung open and Win walked into the room that she forced her scattering thoughts back into a pattern she could identify.

That pattern filled her with irritation.

"Win! What do you think you are doing just walking into my room? I could have been getting dressed, or something."

His brow lifted in sardonic amusement. "Since we know the only 'or something' you are going to be engaging in will be with me and you are still decently covered, you might as well relax, honey."

She shot to her feet, channeling all her tumultuous thoughts into the safer venue of anger. "That's not the point and you know it. I am your employee, not your wife, and I deserve some privacy."

His frown at the word wife only underscored the differences between them. "Listen, honey, right now you're a woman that has me tied up in knots. I'm definitely not thinking of you as my employee."

She crossed her arms under her chest. "Well, maybe you should and save us both a lot of trouble."

He shook his head. "Uh uh. It isn't going to work. You aren't built anything like my other employees."

"Just what is that supposed to mean?"

He made a placating gesture with his hand. "Calm down, Carlene. I didn't come in here to start the next range war."

She harrumphed. "Then why did you come in here?"

His sigh would have parted her hair if he were two feet closer. "I came to invite you to join me for a nightcap."

CHAPTER EIGHT

CARLENE'S eyes filled with shock. "A nightcap? You want me to come have a drink with you?"

Her voice came out a high squeak and Win wondered why she sounded so disbelieving. She didn't think he was going to let her get away with avoiding him for ever, did she? They had things to work out and that wasn't going to happen with her hiding in her bedroom every time the kids were asleep.

"I opened a bottle of wine and it's waiting in the living room." That should please her. Women thought wine was romantic. Given his choice, he would have preferred a nice glass of Macallan scotch on the rocks.

"I don't think that's a good idea. We both have to get up early and Shelly will probably wake up again in the middle of the night, needing to be rocked back to sleep. I don't want to miss hearing her because I've anesthetized my brain with alcohol. We've just had ice cream. It isn't a good idea to mix alcohol with a big sugar rush, I'm sure." She talked so fast, she sounded like the auctioneer for the Cattleman's Association annual fundraiser.

Maybe she thought if she said it fast enough, he wouldn't find her excuses downright bizarre. He laughed out loud. "Honey, you're being ridiculous. One glass of wine isn't going to dull your senses to the point that you won't hear Shelly if she wakes up. As for mixing sugar and alcohol—"

She didn't let him finish. "Never mind that. We both still have to get up early. I need my sleep. You said so this afternoon."

She stood next to her bed, her hair a wild mass around her shoulders, looking triumphant. She thought she'd made an iron-clad argument. He reached for her and hooked her wrist. If he didn't get her out of the vicinity of her bed very soon, he'd be making his arguments with his body, not his mouth.

"You can take a nap while the kids are sleeping again tomorrow, if you want. It's not that late and I want some company," he said as he pulled her from the room.

"So, what you want is all that matters?" She lowered her voice as he pulled her past the kids' door.

He sighed with irritation as he pulled her down the stairs to the courtyard. She gave a low exclamation.

He turned around. "What's the matter?"

She glared at him, her face illuminated by moonlight. "I stepped on something."

He looked down at her feet and realized for the first time that she'd already taken off her shoes. If he'd waited a few more minutes to come to her room, there was a strong possibility he would have found her already undressed. The thought was too damned tempting to contemplate for very long. He swung her up into his arms. This time instead of fighting him, she put her arms around his neck and held on.

He liked this way a whole lot better.

He carried her through the courtyard into the living room and reluctantly let her go. Turning to the tray he had brought in before going to get Carlene, he asked, "Wine okay?"

"I suppose I should be grateful you didn't throw me over you shoulder and carry me in here like a sack of potatoes again," she said, her feisty nature asserting itself.

He remained silent, waiting for an answer to his earlier question.

She sighed. "Wine is fine."

He poured the golden liquid into a wineglass and handed it to her. "Let's get something straight. I didn't carry you like a sack of potatoes last time and I sure as certain didn't put you over my shoulder. Got that?"

She looked taken aback by his vehemence. Too bad. He was tired of everybody and his mother telling him he'd manhandled her. She'd been a whole lot more squirmy on the first trip through the courtyard in his arms, but she had in no way resembled a sack of potatoes.

"Got it," she said.

"Good. Now, drink your wine."

She sat down in an overstuffed chair that matched the leather sofa. Her choice amused him. Did she think if she sat on the couch, he'd seduce her? Even funnier, did she believe that sitting in a chair was going to stop him? He poured himself a glass of wine and sat on the sofa where it rested kitty corner to her chair. He stretched his legs out in front of him. She shifted hers a few inches to the left so they wouldn't touch.

Taking a sip of her wine, she looked at him over the rim of her glass. "Did anyone ever tell you that charm is not your strong suit?"

He felt a slow smile grow on his face. The woman sure could put her tongue to good use. "Now that you mention it, Leah has said something a time or two about my lack of tact."

She looked thoughtful for a moment. "I suppose that doesn't bother you?"

The question surprised him. "What?"

"Having others think less of you."

"My sister doesn't think less of me because I don't attend to every social nicety."

Carlene's gaze traveled around the room before coming back to settle on him. "No, I don't suppose she does."

They were both silent for a minute.

"It bothers me, you know," she said.

"What bothers you?" he asked. Her pensive mood confused him after her earlier nervousness, but he wasn't going to discourage it. Maybe he'd finally get the answers about her past that he'd been wanting.

"Having others think less of me. Having them believe the worst of me, particularly those I care about and respect."

"Who thought the worst of you, honey?"

Her eyes focused on something that he could not see. Perhaps the past. "When I graduated from high school, I knew just what I wanted, to be a teacher. So, I took an accelerated masters program. I was twenty-three when I finished my practicum and got my first real job teaching. I was offered a position at the high school near my hometown." She let out a long breath. "Maybe I was too young to teach high school, too close to the kids in age. I don't know."

The image of Carlene teaching fit his view of her a whole lot better than her working at the Dry Gulch. Despite the fact she was working as his housekeeper, he wasn't really surprised by her true profession. He wanted to know why she wasn't teaching now, though.

When she didn't go on, he asked an innocuous question he hoped would open her up further. "What did you teach?"

For a moment, her concentration returned to him. "English Lit."

He took a sip of his wine. It wasn't that bad. "Not my favorite subject."

She smiled, her expression indulgent. "I understand. It isn't everybody's, but I loved it. I still do."

"What happened?" Something pretty serious for her to end up his housekeeper, cook and nanny.

An expression of pain flitted across her face as her eyes lost focus again. "The first year was great. I established a strong rapport with my students and the rest of the faculty seemed to like me."

"The second year things changed?" he guessed.

"Yes. Our principal retired. The new one the district hired was really different. His methods and attitudes didn't mesh with my own. We had a few dust-ups, but nothing I couldn't handle until he decided that I would make a good after-school buddy."

Fury washed through Win before he had a chance to fully digest her words. "He made a pass at you?"

"You could say that. He was much too smart to do anything for which I could accuse him of sexual harassment. He made several innuendos, brushed up against me when we passed in the halls, things like that."

"The bastard."

She took a long drink of her wine and then wiped the back of her mouth with her hand. "My sentiments exactly. The worst part was that he was married to one of the sweetest women I'd ever met. It made everything ten times worse. Finally, one day he made a comment that I couldn't ignore and I let him know in no uncertain terms that I wasn't interested."

"Like you did with Lonny?" He could just see the resulting scandal if the English Lit teacher got caught punching the principal of the local high school.

She smiled ruefully. "Not that drastic, but he got the picture. Things got worse after that. He questioned my decisions, dropped in unannounced on my classes. He said he was checking up on me, making sure there were no discipline problems. All of a sudden he had a problem with a single woman my age teaching high school. I still thought I could handle it. I was such a fool."

The defeat and self-condemnation in her voice touched a chord deep inside him. He knew what it meant to play the part of the fool. "What happened?"

"I had the star quarterback in my third-period class. He was a smart boy, but he skimmed on his work. I made the mistake of grading him according to the work he turned in to my class and not on his football-playing ability."

Win had heard stories of teachers being forced to alter grades for star athletes. "You tried to flunk him?"

"He failed one assignment. With his other low grades, that put his playing for the school team at risk." She crossed one green-denim-clad leg over the other. "The principal tried to get me to give him a passing grade."

He thought he knew what was coming. "You wouldn't back down."

"No." The single word said it all. Carlene wouldn't lie for anyone. Her personal code of honor was too high.

"So, they removed him from your class?"

She gave a short bitter laugh. "If only it had been that easy. The student filed a harassment charge against me. He said I'd made a play for him and flunked him when he refused to have anything to do with me."

Cold anger surged through Win. If that lying little weasel had been within spitting distance, Win would have made sure he wasn't up to playing quarterback for a very long time, if ever.

Unaware of the rage pulsing through him, Carlene went on. "It was ridiculous and I didn't take it very seriously at first. I assumed no one would believe him. I was wrong."

He couldn't stand it any longer. Needing to comfort the pain he heard in her voice, Win pulled her gently from her chair into his arms.

She was stiff at first, but suddenly she just snuggled against him and spoke into his chest. "It was horrible. Everyone gossiped about me and somehow my looks and my body were considered the measure of my morality rather than my personality or past. I got calls in the middle of the night making threats and accusing me of things I hadn't even heard of. My principal asked me to resign."

He rubbed her back with continuous downward strokes. "What did you do?"

"I refused to resign. I fought back. I still had my grading records and the last assignment that clearly deserved a failing grade. I hired a lawyer who took depositions on my behalf. He was able to prove the spuriousness of the student's claim. We'd never been in the same room alone."

Win sensed that wasn't the end of the story. If it had been, she would still be in west Texas teaching high school.

"If the principal had stood behind you, things would have been a lot better," he said, trying to get a feel for the rest of the story.

"Yes. It would have. However, he was the one that insisted on opening a full-scale investigation—even after the boy admitted he'd made it up to get on the team."

The yellow-bellied snake. "You were acquitted."

She pulled back so that she could see his face. What he saw on hers made him tighten his hold on her. Her eyes mirrored a wound that was not completely healed.

"In the eyes of the law, absolutely, but not that town. The day I won the case, I went to my parents' house. They were about the only two people in town I was certain were still speaking to me."

"Did they celebrate your victory with you?" He had to ask, although the truth was there in her eyes.

She surprised him when she said, "Sort of."

Maybe it wasn't that bad, but his gut told him it was.

Her lip trembled and she took a calming breath before going on. "They congratulated me on winning the case, but my dad suggested I look for a job somewhere else. He said he wanted me to have a new start. To get away from the gossip, but I realized that a good deal of his motivation was that he and mom had been humiliated by my problems and they wanted peace in their lives again. Mom told me later that some of Dad's golfing buddies had refused to play with him any longer. She said their friends had been pressuring them to get me to leave town."

Win couldn't believe the lack of loyalty and weakness her parents had shown. How had they managed to raise a woman as strong and dependable as Carlene? But then, his mom had raised him, hadn't she? "Did your mom want you to leave town?"

"Yes, but she was a little more subtle. She suggested I take a vacation before going back to work."

"A vacation?" he asked.

"She thought I should go to Southern California."

"Why there?"

"Lots of plastic surgeons, or so she had been told."

"So?" He was confused.

"She suggested I get a breast reduction. Apparently women with a figure like mine invite the sort of trouble I had at my school."

Win could not believe her mother had been so incredibly stupid. "It wasn't your fault!"

Her eyes glistened. "Thanks."

"You don't have to thank me for the truth." He'd like some time to talk about the truth with her parents. They certainly didn't deserve a daughter as wonderful as Carlene.

She settled back against his chest. "I decided that Mom and Dad deserved some peace, so I resigned from my position at the high school, packed my car and left."

"You didn't go to California," he said with satisfaction.

He felt her smile against his shirtfront. "No. I won't say I didn't think about it, but I came to the conclusion that I like myself. It wasn't my fault my boss was a lecher or that I had a student with the morals of a bull moose."

He smiled at the return of her feistiness. "You came here instead."

"Sunshine Springs was just a little dot on the map. I liked the name of the town and so I came. Once I got here, I found a job right away, so I decided to stay."

"Not as a teacher."

She grimaced. "No, definitely not as a teacher. But I'm tired of hiding from what might happen. I want to teach again."

"You still want to teach high school?" he asked, awed by her courage.

"You probably think I'm nuts, but yes. I was a good high-school teacher. I want my dreams back. I want my life back. I've let other people, not very nice people, have too much of it as it is."

* * *

The next night, Carlene went looking for Win after she finished tucking the children into bed. She found him down by the stables. He was giving Shorty instructions about one of the pregnant mares.

"Win."

Both he and Shorty turned toward her at the sound of her voice.

Win smiled. "Hi, honey. What do you need?"

"I need to talk to you. Do you have a minute?"

He nodded. "Sure."

Turning to Shorty, Win asked, "You got everything covered here?"

"Yeah, boss."

Win turned and headed toward Carlene and the house.

She watched Shorty go into the building behind Win. "Is Shorty staying the night with the horses?"

Win nodded. "Yeah. One of my mares is ready to foal anytime. He'll call my beeper if she goes into labor."

They went through the house and into the courtyard as if by one accord. Win sat on a chair near the fountain. It was next to the table with the ice tea Carlene had set out in anticipation of their talk. She took the chair on the other side of the small table.

Win picked up one of the glasses and took a long swallow. "What did you want to talk about?" he asked.

"Leah."

His eyes widened. "What about her?"

"When is she coming back, Win?"

He shrugged, as if the answer were of no importance at all. "Soon, I imagine."

She wasn't going to let him sidestep this issue. "When is soon? Tomorrow, the next day, next week?"

His eyes narrowed. "Why are you so interested all of a sudden? You tired of taking care of the kids?"

She didn't like the accusation in his tone. "You know that's not true, but they miss her. It was very difficult to get them both to sleep tonight, but particularly Shelly. She wants her mom."

He looked placated by her answer. "Leah needs some space."

Frustration filled Carlene. "Well, her children need *her*."

"Shelly and Jared will be fine." Win smiled at her. "You're doing great with them."

"I'm not their mom, Win, and that's who they need right now. Leah is going to have to work her problems out with her children around."

Win's expression closed. "Leah knows what is best for her kids. She's a good mother, a better one than she ever had."

Why wouldn't he listen to what Carlene was saying? "I did not mean to imply that I thought anything different. I'm simply pointing out that it's time for Leah to come back."

Win slammed his ice tea down on the table. Brown liquid sloshed over the sides. "You're my housekeeper and the kids' temporary nanny. It's not up to you to tell me what my sister should or should not do."

The attack was so unexpected that it left Carlene speechless.

Win's fury was gone almost as fast as it had come. He reached out and brushed his hand down her arm. "I'm sorry, honey. I didn't mean to snap at you."

She jerked away from his touch. "No problem. I was clearly stepping outside the bounds of our employee-employer relationship by expressing my concern for the two children in my care."

He put his hands on his thighs and blew out a long breath. "I said I was sorry. I know you're worried about the kids, but you've got to trust their mom to know what's best for them."

"Why? Did your mom always know what was best for you? Being a parent doesn't make you infallible."

She'd learned that lesson very well as a teacher.

Win's expression turned dangerous. "Leah is nothing like our mother. She cares more for Jared and Shelly than Mom ever cared for us."

He wasn't shouting, but the cold fury in his voice was just as intimidating.

Carlene refused to back down. "For the second time, I'm not implying that Leah is a poor mother. I am saying that she needs to get back here and comfort her children."

"That's enough." His hands fisted against his thighs. "Leah will get here when she gets here and

until then we will take care of Shelly and Jared.
Understood?"

"Can't we at least contact their father? Maybe
Leah's husband is back from his business trip and
would come get the children."

Win's glare knifed through her with the precision
of a surgeon's scalpel. "Why don't you just come
right out and say it? You're bored watching the kids
and you want a change."

The injustice of the accusation caught her on the
raw. She exploded from her chair and stormed over
to Win. She was so angry she was shaking. Leaning
over him, she found it difficult to control her trembling
limbs. No one had ever made her mad as Win could.

"Listen closely, you stubborn cowboy, because
I've taken about all the insults I'm going to off of
you. I am concerned about Leah's children. I believe
they need their mother. If she won't make herself
available, then we try to find their father. I don't
care if they are used to him being gone for weeks
at a time. He's still their father and having him
around will give them more security than they've
got right now."

She punctuated the last sentence with jabs to
Win's sternum. The cold fury in Win's eyes made her
nervous and she stepped back, but he didn't move.
He just caught her gaze and held it captive with an
intensity that could have been physical.

"We will not call Mark. If my sister says he's out of town, then that is where he is."

Carlene couldn't help trying again. "Maybe he got back early."

"Forget it."

"But, Win—"

He cut her off. "I said forget it and I meant it, Carlene. You are my employee. You have nothing to say in the matter and I damn well don't want to hear anything else on the subject. Leah will be back in a couple of days and then you'll be free from the burden of watching her children. If you don't think you can handle it, I'll find someone else. What's it to be?"

An iron fist squeezed Carlene's heart, making it difficult to breathe past the pain. "I'll watch the children and be your employee, but *nothing more*."

She turned and stumbled toward her bedroom, tears clouding her vision. Blinking furiously, she willed herself not to cry until she had reached the relative safety of her room.

She hadn't reached the inner hallway before strong fingers clamped onto her shoulders from behind, halting her in mid-step. She struggled against his hold. "Let me go!"

"No. I can't."

The raw fear in his voice had barely registered when he spun her around and pulled her into a tight embrace against his chest. "I was wrong, honey. You're more than an employee and we both know it."

She struggled against the strength of his arms and argued against his shirtfront. "No, we don't know it. You don't want my interference and I don't want you. Let me go, Win."

He had to release her before she lost it. The pain in her chest was so tight, she could barely breathe. She'd been falling in love with this man and he wanted sex. Nothing more. Not her concern for the children. Not her interference in his life. Nothing, but her body. And she didn't know how to give only that. If she ever let Win make love to her, she'd give him everything and she knew it.

Frantic to get him to let her go, she swung her foot forward and kicked his shin. "Let me loose."

He grunted, but his hold didn't so much as loosen a fraction of an inch. Her toes felt as if they had a run-in with a cement wall.

"Please, Carlene, you've got to listen to me."

She threw her head back so she could glare up into his face. "Like you listened to me?"

"I made a mistake. I'm sorry. Give me a chance to make it right."

"Why? So you can come to my bed? You don't really care that you've hurt me. You don't care what I think about your sister, or her children, or how much they're hurting. You're just trying to placate me so I'll let you seduce me, but it's not going to happen. I've been an idiot, but I won't be one any longer."

Blue eyes shot fire at her. "No. Damn it. That's not the way it is."

"Oh, really?" she asked with as much sarcasm as she could put into the two words. "Then how is it? Are you going to deny that you want me?"

His grip on her tightened. "Hell, no. I want you so much that I spend most of the time when I'm with you damned uncomfortable in my pants, but that isn't why I apologized."

"Then why?"

"Because I was wrong. Because I can't stand hurting you. Because your opinion matters to me and I'm sorry I went ballistic on you. Truly, deeply sorry. Please, honey, don't walk away from me."

"Let me go." She said it quietly, but he listened this time.

He released her with obvious reluctance. "Come back and sit down. Please," he said again. "We'll talk this out."

CHAPTER NINE

CARLENE shook her head. "Talk what out? You've already informed me that I have nothing to say in this matter. I can't imagine what we've got to discuss."

Win surprised her by smiling, though it looked ragged around the edges. "Honey, the day you have nothing to say about something is the day I'll be rushing you to the emergency room worried about the condition of your vocal cords. Besides, I *also* said your opinion matters to me."

"If I say something you don't like, are you going to yell at me again?" she demanded quietly.

"No," he put up his hand. "Scouts' honor."

Some of the tension drained from her. If he was willing to talk rationally, then she could too. She returned to her seat near the fountain. Win joined her. She waited in silence, sipping at her ice tea. If he thought she was going to reopen the subject after the way he'd shot her down, he didn't know her very well.

Win took a deep breath and let it out slowly. Then

he turned to her. "I've been protecting my baby sister since my mom brought her home from the hospital when I was five years old. I'm a little sensitive when I think someone else is criticizing her, I guess."

Carlene raised her brows. "You don't say?"

Win frowned. "Look, I'm trying to explain and I've already said I was sorry. Cut me a little slack."

He'd done more than apologize. He'd begged. She could do as he asked.

"You don't explain yourself very often, do you?" she asked.

"No. I don't." He ran his fingers through his black hair. "What I'm trying to say is that I understand your concerns. I know the kids miss her. It scares the hell out of me that she left them here. I don't know what's going on with her and Mark."

"You're afraid that she's like your mother and that's why you overreacted when I expressed my concern."

Once she'd said the words, Carlene waited, barely breathing, to see how Win would react to them.

He rubbed a hand across his eyes. "Yes."

The word was a bare whisper of sound.

"Listen to me, Win. Leah is not your mother. Whatever is going on in her head right now must be pretty devastating, or she wouldn't have left her children."

His eyes pleaded with her. "How do you know? You've never even met her."

"Shelly and Jared are too well adjusted and loving

for her to be anything but a terrific mother. Win, you do know her and you know she isn't like your mom."

"You're right, but then what is the point of the things you said earlier?"

She knew her smile was tinged with exasperation. He really didn't get it. "The point of what I was trying to say is that I think you should tell your sister to come back or call her husband. Shelly and Jared need their parents."

"I don't want to call Mark."

"Why?" she asked.

"I don't think he knows that Leah left the kids with me. If I call him, it could cause problems in their marriage," Win said.

"It sounds like there are already problems, or Leah wouldn't be having the crisis she's having right now."

Win nodded. "I know, but if she has some time alone, maybe she'll get over wanting to leave him. She doesn't need me calling him and making things worse."

"You really are afraid that she's like your mom, aren't you? Win, you've got to accept that if Leah is thinking about leaving Mark, she's got solid reasons. She's too committed a parent to divorce him on a whim and I think deep down you know that."

Win's expression relaxed a little. "Yes. I do know that. Hell, I don't even know if she's thinking about divorce. She just told me she needed some time to think. When I talked to her on the phone the other day, I could tell that she misses the kids as much as they miss her. I don't know what's going on."

Carlene understood Win's quandary. He didn't want to cause more ripples in a marriage that might already be on the brink and he was confused by his sister's behavior. From everything he'd said and the impression Carlene got from others, it was entirely out of character.

"Do you have a phone number for her for emergencies?" she asked Win.

"Yes. She really is a good mother, Carlene."

"I believe you. She isn't going to mind you calling her and telling her that her children need her. Maybe that's something *she* needs to hear right now."

He stood up. "You're right. Guess I'll go call her before it gets too late."

Carlene watched him go, her heart aching for the pain both he and Leah were suffering right now. Carlene had no doubt that Leah was just as terrified as Win that she was like their mother.

Carlene carried the ice tea glasses into the kitchen and wondered if Win would come looking for her after he had spoken to Leah. Would he understand that Carlene was anxious to know the outcome of the telephone conversation?

More importantly, would he want to share it with her as a man shared important things with a woman who was more than just an employee?

* * *

Win sat down in his chair and stared at the number he'd written on a slip of paper by the phone. Carlene was right. He knew it. He had to call Leah. If for nothing else, but to make sure that she was okay. He inhaled deeply, trying to gather his thoughts. He wanted to express his concern for the kids without making Leah feel worse than she already did. It wasn't going to be easy.

He wished that he'd shown the same forethought before running off at the mouth at Carlene. He'd hurt her. When she went running from the courtyard, he'd been filled with fear. Part of him had known that if he let her go without making things right, he would lose his chance with her. She was already fighting a relationship with him for all she was worth.

His idiotic comment that she was no more than an employee would give her ammunition in the war she waged against becoming his lover. He couldn't risk losing her. So he had done something he rarely did—apologized. Then he'd tried to explain. That hadn't been easy. He didn't like analyzing his emotions and he hated talking about the past, but she needed to understand why he'd been so defensive.

He didn't know if she forgave him completely, but she had listened. She hadn't pouted and she'd comforted him.

She had been right. He was afraid that Leah was turning out like their mother. Carlene's assertion that if his sister was considering ending her marriage, she'd have a darn good reason, rang true. Leah loved Mark. She loved her kids and she wasn't just bored. Something was going on. Something serious. Win just wished he knew what it was.

He picked up the phone and dialed.

Carlene checked the clock on the bedside table for the third time in fifteen minutes. She had left her door cracked open so that Win wouldn't assume she was asleep, but an hour had passed and he still hadn't come. Could his conversation with Leah have lasted this long? Doubt gnawed at her. Maybe he didn't see Carlene as someone with whom he could or should share his family's problems.

She'd pinned her hopes on the fact that he apologized for his outburst. She had believed he was truly sorry for hurting her, for implying she had no place in his life outside that of employee and perhaps casual bed partner.

The soft knock sent hope surging through her. Jumping up off the bed, she called, "Come in."

Win pushed the door open wider and stepped inside. His face wore a more relaxed expression than she'd seen all evening. He smiled. "Hi. Mind if I come in and talk for a while?"

Win in an asking mood pushed her a little off center.

She indicated the chair and ottoman in the corner. "Uh, take a seat."

He pulled the ottoman away from the chair and straddled it, putting his hands on his knees.

She edged around him and sat on the chair. "So how did the call to your sister go?" she asked, impatient to hear the details.

"You were right. She needed to hear that the kids missed her. She'd gotten some crazy ideas in her head."

"Like what?" Carlene asked.

"Like her husband and children didn't really need her. That she was just a glorified housekeeper and nanny. Crazy stuff like that."

"She must really be hurting."

Win's expression turned to one of concern. "Yeah. I think she is. She and Mark need to talk. I told her that."

"You did?" Carlene couldn't hide the surprise in her voice. Win was not what one would consider a modern male with sensitivity training.

"Yeah, I did. You don't have to be a pop psychologist to know that a married couple needs to talk out their problems," he said, indicating he had guessed her thoughts.

She smiled. "No. You don't. When is she coming back?"

"It could be as early as tomorrow. I told her not to rush, but that the kids would be real happy when she got here."

He had said it just right. "You're a nice man, Win."

"If you believe that, why won't you go to bed with me?"

After she recovered from the shock of his blunt query, Carlene frowned. "Don't tell me that tactless questions like that have gotten you past first base before."

Win grinned. "I haven't dated all that many women, but the ones I did didn't seem to be bothered by my 'lack of tact'."

Irritation at the mention of women in Win's past made Carlene reckless. "What about your ex-wife? Did she have a problem with your lack of tact?"

She regretted the words the moment they left her mouth. She wished with all her heart she could call them back when Win's expression of amused tolerance turned cold and stony. Darn it.

When would she learn to control her tongue? "I'm sorry I asked that."

"Why? Don't you want an answer?" His voice held no inflection, as if the discussion had no importance for him. His eyes told another story.

"I don't want you to feel obligated to tell me anything you don't want to." Of course she wanted to know about his ex-wife. What woman in Carlene's position wouldn't want to know about the one female that Win had been willing to take the risk of marriage on?

He contemplated her answer for several long seconds. She began to fidget, shifting nervously in her chair. Resting his elbows on his thighs, he leaned forward and examined her eyes.

Like a jackrabbit who sensed the presence of a predator, her entire body went still. What was he thinking? He kept his gaze fixed on her so long that the sound of his voice surprised her when he spoke.

"By the time she left me, Rachel let me know that she pretty much hated everything about me, my lack of tact included."

Impossible. No woman could hate everything about this man. He had too much loyalty, too much honor; too much of what made a man a good man.

She instinctively shook her head. "She must have been crazy."

He didn't smile. He didn't even blink. "Not crazy. Determined. She wanted out of this little hole-in-the-wall town and she thought I was her ticket out of here."

Carlene's chest tightened. "I don't understand."

"It's simple. Rachel married me, believing she could convince me to sell the ranch and stake her life in the big city. When she discovered that I had no desire to uproot Leah's new life, or my own, Rachel made it clear that she found me lacking in just about everything. I wore my boots too scuffed and my hair too long. According to her, I was rude and uncouth. Toward the end, she couldn't even stand me touching her at night. Not that I wanted to all that much. The town was just starting to attract a certain clientele for winter sports. She hitched her star to one of their hangers-on and left Sunshine Springs behind just like she wanted."

Pain for Win's loss ripped through Carlene. His marriage sounded more like a civil war.

"How long were you married?" She almost asked how long he'd had to endure Rachel.

"Less than two years."

"All of that happened in less than two years?" She couldn't keep the disbelief from her voice.

His grim features relaxed into a smile. "Yeah. One thing you can say for me, when I screw up, I do it fast and well."

Carlene could not digest his attitude. "You didn't screw up. You married her believing she wanted the same things from life that you did. It's hardly your fault she lied to you. You must have loved her very much."

"I married her because I wanted a woman's touch raising Leah and because I was tired of walking around with a perpetual hard-on. I told you, she made me wait for sex until we got married. I thought she was just an old-fashioned girl. Hell, she wasn't even a virgin."

The self-disgust in Win's voice tore at Carlene's defenses. "Win, there's nothing wrong with your wanting a woman to help Leah through the difficult years of adolescence. It's unfortunate that Rachel wasn't interested in making you a proper wife or your sister a suitable mentor."

He stared at her as if she had just spoken in Portuguese. "Well, at least now you understand why I'm not going to jump into the trap of marriage again."

The certainty in his voice crushed the hope that

had been blossoming since Win knocked on her bedroom door. How could she prove to him that marriage didn't have to be a trap if he wouldn't take a chance on it, on her? She needed more time than a short-term affair provided to prove that she wasn't like his mother. Carlene wouldn't get bored with him after six months.

If he wouldn't risk a committed relationship with her, how could Carlene show him that she wasn't like Rachel either? She didn't want him to give up his life and his roots in the community to make her happy and she knew that she would never grow immune to his touch. She couldn't. She loved him.

There was no point in denying the truth any longer. She was crazy in love with the stubborn, sexy rancher and her life was never going to be the same.

"I understand that you got burned and that you are leery of committing yourself to another woman."

He leaned further forward until his blue eyes burned into her own. "Listen to me, Carlene. Listen close. I'm not just leery. I am not interested in marriage."

He spoke each word with precision, leaving her in no doubt that he meant exactly what he said. She would have to be a fool to believe that she might be able to change his mind. The earlier recklessness she had experienced returned. So what? Men and women had been doing foolish things in the name of love throughout history and it didn't always end in heart-ache. Sometimes love conquered.

She had to believe that this would be one of those times. She couldn't accept the alternative—a future without Win.

She reached out and wrapped her fingers around one of his fists. "But, you are interested in me."

He closed his eyes, his expression that of a man in pain. "Yes, honey. I want you so much it's killing me."

She believed him.

Reaching out with her other hand, she traced the line of his jaw. "Where will we end up in that whole range of possibilities between a one-night stand and marriage that you told me about?"

His eyes flew open and she felt his muscles go battle-ready under her fingertips. "Are you saying that you're willing to give us a try?"

How odd that he would put it in those terms. To her way of thinking, it had been Win who refused to give them a chance. He didn't see things that way. The knowledge gave her hope.

"Maybe. I can't promise anything, Win. You have to tell me where we'll fit on that spectrum of possibilities first."

He turned his face and kissed the palm of her hand that rested against his cheek. "I guess just taking it one day at a time won't work for you?"

She shook her head. "I need some assurance that I'm not simply a convenient body."

He laughed, relieving some of the pent-up tension

between them. "Honey, you are a ways from being convenient. That's for damn sure."

She didn't return his smile. She couldn't. She had to know the answer. "Then what am I?"

She was giving up her dreams to go back to teaching school for a chance with Win. A small town like Sunshine Springs was never going to hire an ex-bartender who was living with her lover to teach their children. She could practice discretion, she supposed, but doubted that would last very long. Besides, she didn't want to hide her love for Win from the rest of the world. She had the feeling that he needed her public commitment as much as she needed to know where she stood with him.

"You're my woman."

She digested that. "For how long?"

His eyes widened in shock. "You want me to put a time limit on our relationship?"

"No."

"Then what do you want?" Frustration radiated off him in waves.

What did she want? Some sort of commitment. A promise, but not marriage. She didn't know. "You're the one that said there's all sorts of ground between a one-night stand and marriage. I just want to know what ground we're talking about. Is that so much to ask?"

"There *is* a lot of ground between the two. I've just

never had to define it before," he said with exasperation.

Dread snaked through her. She pulled her hands from him and scooted back in the large chair. "Have you had a lot of situations where you might have had to, but they didn't ask?"

If she sounded confused, that was only fair. After all, she *felt* confused.

"No! I told you. There haven't been *that* many women."

"Believe it or not, your attitude is not helping to set my mind at ease," she replied, her own frustration lacing her words.

He smiled ruefully. "Look, honey, I don't have a string of lovers in my past. It's been so long since my last date that Shorty was starting to get worried."

Somewhat mollified, she nodded. "Okay, then. I can see that defining what our relationship is might be a little difficult for you. You obviously need some time to think about it."

He swore. "You aren't going to let me make love to you tonight, are you?"

She stood and indicated the door with her hand. "You need time and I'm willing to give it to you. Goodnight, Win. Go get some sleep."

He didn't go. He stood too and towered over her, his entire body emanating male desire. He fixed her with a piercing blue gaze and settled his hands on her shoulders, the heat of his fingers burning through the cloth of her shirt.

"What I need right now, honey, is you. The question is, are you ready to put me out of my misery?"

CHAPTER TEN

CARLENE shivered at the suppressed desire in Win's voice.

Was she willing to put him out of his misery? Was she willing to risk letting him make love to her without defining their relationship?

His face took on a serious, almost feral, expression. "I don't know the *words* for what we have, but I can show you, if you'll let me."

She couldn't speak. She wanted him so much and suddenly the idea of talking didn't hold all that much appeal. He didn't want marriage, but he did want her. Not a nameless, faceless woman to warm his body, but *her.* And she loved him.

In all her dreams of love and a family, they never included this desperate edgy feeling. This despair and pain mixed with joy and desire. They might not be married, but she knew with every pulse of her heart that she belonged to him. Completely. Her heart. Her body. Her desire. They were all his. If she refused to let him make love to her, that would not change. If he made love to her tonight and then walked away tomorrow, that still wouldn't change the truth of her love.

She loved him.

She needed him.

She *wanted* him.

His thumbs brushed the sensitive skin of her neck up to the underside of her chin. "Please. Let me make you mine tonight."

For the second time that night, her proud, arrogant cowboy was reduced to pleading with her.

She reached up and curled her fingers over his wrists, awed by the strength that held her so gently. "Yes, Win."

His eyes turned stormy blue and his nostrils contracted. He didn't waste time asking if she were sure or saying anything else at all. He closed the distance between their mouths and locked his over hers in a possessive kiss that shook her to her toes. Flicking his tongue over the seam of her lips, he silently demanded entry into her mouth.

She gave it without so much as a thought.

She expected him to sweep her mouth with branding passion, but, from the moment he entered her mouth, his kiss gentled. He explored her with lazy thoroughness letting her adjust to his possession while she relearned his taste.

Wanting more, but not knowing how to get it, she

released his wrists and tunneled her fingers into the black silk of his hair. She tugged against his head while trying to press her body against his. The hold on her shoulders prevented her. She moaned in protest.

Now that she'd decided to make love to Win, she wanted it all. Immediately.

He refused to be rushed and kept going with that slow, tantalizing kiss. Heavens, the man knew how to use his mouth to advantage. Her nipples grew tight and aching, though he hadn't so much as touched them. The confines of her bra and shirt seemed too much all of a sudden. She wanted them off.

Now.

She tried to let Win know without breaking that incredible kiss. She squirmed. She made needy little sounds low in her throat, but she couldn't make herself break contact with his lips. Maybe if she touched him, he'd get the idea.

Reluctantly, she slid her fingers from his hair; mourning the loss of one erotic touch even as she lowered her hands to grasp his shirt near the waist-band of his jeans. She tugged until she could get her hands under the hem. She brushed his stomach and the muscles under her fingers tightened convulsively.

Win growled and let go of her shoulders to yank her closer, trapping her hands between their bodies. The relief of having her breasts crushed against the work-hardened muscles of his chest was short-lived. It just wasn't enough.

She wanted skin on skin, but couldn't even move her hands against the bare skin of belly, he held her so tight.

She forced herself to tear her mouth from his. "Please, Win. I need… I want…" She couldn't make herself say it.

She'd never made love with a man. Her experiences with Win were the closest she'd ever come and she didn't know how to tell him she wanted him to touch her body.

He rocked against her, sending jolts of pleasure rocketing through her feminine core. "What do you want, baby? Tell me."

"I can't," she wailed.

He let his hands slide down to cup her bottom and squeezed.

Oh, my goodness, that felt good.

"Sure you can, honey. Tell me what you want."

She shook her head, but he ignored the refusal and just kept tormenting her with almost touches. He'd press his erection against the juncture of her thighs and then pull back. One erotic squeeze of her bottom and then his hands would move back up to knead her back. All the while he kept her hands trapped against heated, tantalizing flesh.

"I want you to touch me like you did in the courtyard," she finally blurted out when she could take no more of his teasing. Once she got started, she couldn't stop. "I want you to take off my top and my bra and touch my breasts. With your hands and your mouth.

I want you touch me between my legs. Only this time, I won't make you stop. I want to touch you too."

She brushed her thumbs up and down, moving them as much as the tight position they were in would allow. His arms tightened around her and he groaned.

"That's good because I want to do all those things and more."

More? What more? She almost asked him, but decided she probably wasn't prepared for the answer. She'd let him show her. *"Then do it,"* she all but shouted.

He chuckled. "You'd better keep it down, honey."

She stifled a scream of mounting frustration.

And then she forgot her frustration as Win pulled away and started undressing her. He tugged off her top, pulling it over her head and letting it fall to the floor.

When he'd looked at her before, there had only been the illumination of moonlight. Now they were in her room with both the overhead light and the lamp on. Embarrassment heated her skin. She wanted his touch, but she didn't want him looking at her. She crossed her arms over her chest and gazed fixedly at the black T-shirt covering his torso.

"Look at me, baby." The words were spoken soft and low, but held such an unmistakable air of authority that she raised her head.

His eyes were midnight blue pools of wanting. "I want to see you. Will you let me?"

She nodded her head, but still didn't move her arms.

He waited.

She chewed on her lip. "Could we turn off the lights?"

He shook his head, but said, "I'll compromise."

And he walked over to flip down the switch for the overhead light, leaving the room bathed in the soft yellow glow from the reading lamp by the bed.

Then he waited. Right where he was. On the other side of the room and somehow the distance between them gave her the courage to lower her arms.

His focus did not at first waver from her face and she was grateful. "Are you okay?"

She nodded, mute.

"Good." Then he let his gaze slide down and she felt as if he were touching her breasts with his fingertips.

Her nipples, already tight, puckered further against the lace of her bra.

"Take it off," he demanded in a guttural voice.

Taking a deep breath, she reached behind and unhooked the clasp of her bra. Then, shrugging her shoulders, she let it fall to the carpet with her shirt.

His breathing turned shallow and raspy. "I'm really glad you didn't listen to your mom."

For a minute his words confused her and then she remembered telling him about her mom suggesting a breast reduction. "They're not *that* big." And they weren't. Certainly not large enough to justify surgery, even if she'd agreed with her mom.

"They're perfect."

She felt her mouth tip in a smile and for the first time she was glad her body was built like a center-fold instead of a schoolmarm. "Thank you."

His hands fisted and then relaxed at his side as if he wanted to reach out and touch her, but had stopped himself.

"Your turn. Take off your T-shirt." She waited to see if he would comply.

He did. With a sexy smile that made her toes curl into the carpet. He did it slowly, revealing an inch of his rock-hard chest at a time until he finally pulled the black knit over his head and tossed it aside. The partial striptease had a direct effect on the spot between her legs and she could *feel* herself growing wetter.

"Now your pants," he said.

She thought about refusing, unsure if she could strip for him, but then realized that he would remove his too and the anticipation of watching such a spec-tacle made up her mind for her. She unsnapped her jeans and following his lead, unzipped her fly one little centimeter at a time. By the time she had the zipper down and had started pushing the waistband over her hips, Win had a fine sheen of sweat on his body.

He swallowed convulsively as she pushed the colored denim completely down her legs and kicked it away. She stood naked except for the silky panties covering her most feminine place. Could he see how wet they were?

"Now you."

He didn't make her say it again, or explain what she meant. He had to take off his boots first. Then his socks. The only sound in the room was their breathing as he unbuttoned his placket one brass button at a time until he could pull the worn blue denim completely off. He wore knit boxers that fit like a second skin, outlining the awesome length and breadth of his erection.

She knew she didn't have a lot of experience with men, had never actually seen a man's engorged penis up close, but he looked big. Really big. Being inquisitive by nature, she'd seen pictures and none of them had prepared her for Win in the flesh.

She swallowed and then licked her lips, unable to break her gaze away from his manhood.

Laughter rumbled in his chest. "You look like you're staring down a bobcat, hoping it won't attack, baby."

The sound of his voice broke her reverie and she looked up to meet amused blue eyes. "I sort of feel like it, if you want the truth."

All amusement melted from his expression. "I'm not going to hurt you, baby." Then he grimaced. "At least no more than absolutely necessary. I've heard it isn't a picnic the first time for a woman."

"You've never made love to a virgin before?" Only the Lord knew why, but that knowledge comforted her.

"No, but I'll take care of you. I promise."

"I believe you, Win. I trust you."

He nodded. "Good." Then he smiled. "Enough to take off those sexy little panties?"

Her hands shook as she gave him her answer with action. Hooking her thumbs in the side elastic, she shimmied the silk down her hips until it slipped off and landed in a puddle at her feet. She stepped out of it.

He didn't wait for her to remind him it was his turn before following suit. Once his boxers were off, his erection jutted out from his body in imposing, bold glory. Bending down, he drew a foil packet from the pocket of his jeans and she wanted to tell him not to bother, but the dream for marriage and a family was hers. He didn't share it and for just a moment pain cut through her excitement.

Then he ripped open the packet and slid the protection over his hardness, bringing her attention back to his manhood. Somehow *that* was supposed to fit inside of her. She didn't see how it could be possible, but she'd read romance novels. She wasn't a complete innocent. Women stretched to accommodate their lovers, or so she'd read. She sure hoped that part of the romance wasn't fantasy.

He put his hand out. "Come here, baby."

She knew what he was asking. He wanted her to trust him. To come to him and show him that she knew she belonged to him. The message was in his eyes as his hand reached toward her. Without conscious volition, her feet started to move toward him, taking the rest of her body with them.

When she reached him, he bent down and kissed her lips with surprising force.

"You belong to me."

"Yes." She couldn't deny it and even if she had, he would know the truth.

He swung her up into his arms, high against his chest, and carried her to the bed. "Hold my neck."

She did and he released her back in order to pull back the bedspread, blanket and sheet.

Then he laid her with infinite care onto the cool sheet of the bed. She didn't release his neck and he came down on top of her, allowing her to feel the entire length of his body against her own for a full minute before rolling to the side. She protested the lack of contact with a soft murmur that turned into a moan as his hand cupped her breast.

Then he touched her, just as he had in the courtyard, only this time she felt as if each whisper of his fingertips were a branding iron making her more completely his. His hands would not leave behind any marks, except on her heart, but she would be his all the same.

And she would make him hers. She would brand him with her touch so that he would never be able to find fulfillment with another woman.

She reached out and circled one turgid, small, male nipple. The hand on her breast tightened. Pleased with that response, she leaned forward and made the same circling motion, only this time with her tongue. He groaned and she did it again. Then, because she couldn't help herself, she took that small, hard nub into her mouth and sucked.

He shouted her name and pushed her away. "No more of that. I'm hanging on by a thread here, baby, and I can't handle any more assaults from that talented little mouth of yours."

She didn't argue, but she had every intention of assaulting him all over his body. Later. Right after she caught her breath from the feelings coursing through her as his mouth closed over her nipple. He suckled her softly at first, his hand on her other nipple, gently rolling it between thumb and forefinger. She squirmed against him and he increased the pressure of both his fingers and his mouth.

The sensation was so exquisite, so overwhelming, she didn't know if she could stand it. Her pelvis rocked off the bed, seeking, needing, wanting. *"Win."*

He sucked harder and she bit back a scream. Then his hand was no longer on her breast, but had slid down her body to claim her feminine flesh. He continued the suckling of her nipple while slipping one hard finger between the folds of her tender flesh. She pushed against that invading finger, until it slid into her wet heat.

Oh, my goodness. Oh, wow. "Win. That's too... It's way more... I can't..." She couldn't finish a sentence to save her life.

It just felt so good. He slid in and out of her tight

channel, stretching the previously untouched flesh, and she almost cried from the wonder of it. Then his thumb pressed between her lips at their apex and made a slow circle around the aroused bud there. She arched off the bed, the sensation so strong that she shook with it.

And a delicious feeling began to throb within her. She felt as if nerve endings attached to her feminine core were radiating outward with a pleasure she'd never known. "Oh, please, oh, please, oh, please. Don't stop. Win. Just don't stop."

And then she was convulsing and crying and shuddering and he wasn't stopping, even when she begged him. Even when it was so intense she thought she'd die from it and then he moved down her body until his mouth was where his thumb had been and he slipped two fingers inside of her. And it felt too tight, but she couldn't make herself say so because his tongue and teeth were touching her intimately and it had begun all over again. This time her body went rigid and then it shook, and shook, and shook. Tears spilled over from her eyes, their damp warmth making tracks down her temples into her hair.

Then she went limp. Unbelievably, bonelessly limp.

He swarmed up her body, laying on top of her, dominating her flesh, though he hadn't yet entered her. His mouth rocked over hers in a claiming kiss, his tongue thrusting inside. She tasted herself and she should have found that distasteful, but she didn't.

She reveled in the carnality of his kiss, in the heated eroticism of his tongue in her mouth.

Then she felt him at the opening of her femininity. The broad head of his penis pushing against her, inexorably. He would take her now and she would welcome him and as he marked her with his body's possession, she would mark him with hers.

It hurt.

It stretched.

"Do you want me to stop?" His voice shook with strain.

"No. Please, Win. Make me yours."

And he did, with one hard, painful thrust. She was so slick from her two orgasms that her body let him in, but she felt stretched to the limit and she lay under him in a state of semi-shock.

He stilled and kissed her again. Soft, comforting kisses. She could feel his entire body tremble from the strain of not moving and yet his kisses held only patient reassurance.

She loved him so much in that moment, the emotion nearly exploded from her chest. She shifted up, just a little bit, to show him that he could move.

He did. Gently stroking in and out. She moaned in a combination of pain and pleasure. His control broke and he thrust in and out of her with hard, decisive thrusts. She cried out, startled by the pain. He stopped and would have drawn out, but she locked her legs around his hips and held him tight.

"No. Don't stop."

The new position opened her more fully to him and relieved some of the pressure between her legs. He must have felt the way her feminine flesh softened around him because he started thrusting again and this time although there was still some discomfort, it felt good too.

He clamped his mouth back over hers and when he came, she absorbed his masculine shout of pleasure. He held her tightly for several minutes after he found his release and then rolled off of her and stood.

He looked down at her thighs. "You bled."

She could see the evidence on him. "A little."

"I'll take care of you." Then he disappeared into the bathroom.

She heard water running and he reappeared a few minutes later, a damp washcloth in his hand. He used it to wash between her thighs and the warmth soothed her flesh. He took it back into the bathroom and then returned to slide into the bed next to her.

She went into his arms without protest, needing the assurance of his touch after the overwhelming events of the night.

Win held Carlene's soft, warm body against his and wondered how in the hell she expected him to define what they'd just done. She'd let him make love to her, had in fact given herself with a sweet generosity that still had him reeling, but he knew she expected him to tell her where their relationship fit between a one-night stand and an affair.

He didn't have the words. Not now. Not when he felt as if his entire world had just been thrust into a new dimension. One that included the knowledge that no other man must ever see Carlene as Win had seen her tonight. All passion and promise.

Tensed for a confrontation, it took him a moment to realize that Carlene was already dozing. Her body lay curled against his in trusting relaxation. She'd tucked her knee between his legs and her hand rested on his chest while she used his shoulder for a pillow, cuddling him as if she'd done it all her life…or would willingly do it for the remainder of his.

Now that he knew about her plans to get back into teaching, his assumption that she was the type of woman to move on didn't hold water. The way she talked, Carlene planned to hang around Sunshine Springs indefinitely. Her commitment to the community was definite.

Was she as committed to him? More importantly, could her commitment to him last for a lifetime?

The questions spinning through his head were interrupted when his beeper went off. The mare must have gone into labor. He gently eased out from Carlene's clinging embrace, taking care not to wake her. He dressed quietly and turned off the lamp before tiptoeing from the room, waiting to put on his boots until he reached outside.

CHAPTER ELEVEN

THE next afternoon, Carlene had just gotten Shelly and Jared down for a nap when the doorbell rang.

She hadn't seen Win all day, but he'd called…just to see how she was. To tell her thank you for last night in a low, gravelly voice that made her wish he were with her in person—and naked. He couldn't leave the stable and things sounded too tense down there for her to offer to bring the kids down to see the horses as she wanted to. With Lonny gone, Win and Shorty had their hands full.

One of the ranch hands had taken food down to the stables at lunchtime and Carlene would have offered to do it, but she didn't want the first time she saw Win after last night to be in front of an audience.

She rushed through the courtyard now to answer the door, wondering who it could be. She didn't think that Leah would bother to ring. Besides, Win wasn't expecting her for another day. Grant had said something about stopping by, but wouldn't he have gone straight down to the stable?

She quit her useless speculation and hurried to the door, wanting to open it before the visitor rang the bell again and perhaps woke one of the children. Carlene swung the door open and stared in open-mouthed amazement at the person standing on the other side.

Zoe Strickland smiled. "Hi. Grant's down at the stable picking Win's brain. I thought I'd come up and say hello to Shelly and Jared."

Carlene forced her mouth to close and then form a somewhat strained smile of greeting. She stepped away from the door. "Come in. Um...the children just went down for their nap. I'm sorry, but I'd prefer not to wake them if you don't mind."

Zoe smiled again. "Of course. Maybe if you're not too busy, we could have some coffee, or something."

Zoe impressed her. A lot. If she was in Zoe's place and someone had tried to seduce Win, she'd want to scratch the woman's eyes out, not invite her to the wedding or drink coffee with her. "Sure. How about iced coffee in the courtyard?"

"That sounds great." Zoe followed Carlene down the hall and out into the courtyard.

"Why don't you wait here while I get the drinks?" Carlene asked. She needed a few moments alone to collect herself.

When she returned, Carlene found Zoe playing

idly with the children's boats in the fountain. Zoe turned when Carlene set the tray down on the wrought iron table. "Shelly and Jared are really special."

"Yes. They are," Carlene agreed.

Zoe sat down. "Leah must be feeling pretty stressed to have left them with Win. I guess you're helping him out?"

Carlene didn't want to gossip, but she didn't see any harm in telling Zoe the circumstances surrounding her watching Leah's children. "Win hired me as his cook and housekeeper a couple of weeks before Leah dropped by with Shelly and Jared. He asked me to add nanny duties to my job description, so here I am."

Zoe smiled. "I don't know Win nearly as well as I know Leah, but I'd say he doesn't ask for much. I'll bet it came out more a command."

Carlene smiled. "You could say that."

"I didn't realize that you wanted to quit your job as a bartender," Zoe said neutrally.

"It didn't fit anymore." Carlene thought of her plans, plans that would go up in smoke if she began an affair with Win, and sighed. She wasn't sure those plans were as important as they once were. When she put them on the scales with a possible future with Win, they didn't weigh as heavily as she thought they would.

Zoe looked at her curiously. "Do you regret it? I imagine you don't make near the money as a house-keeper that you did tending bar."

Carlene smiled wryly. "You're right, but it pays the bills and, no, I don't regret quitting. You're going to find this hard to believe, but working at the Dry Gulch really didn't fit my temperament."

Zoe nodded, but didn't say anything. She relaxed against her chair and took another sip of her drink. "This feels nice. Things have been hectic with Grant making the changes at the ranch and my class's preparations for the spring program at school."

Carlene felt a stab of envy at Zoe's mention of the school program. "Zoe…" She let her words trail off.

Zoe turned her head slightly. "Yes?"

"I just wanted to say that I'm sorry about Grant. I really didn't mean to cause any problems for you two."

Zoe's look was filled with understanding. "I believe you. I think that Grant really deserves the most credit for the snafu, if you want my opinion."

"He gave me roses, I assumed he—"

Zoe nodded. "Exactly. A man shouldn't give flowers to one woman when he wants another."

The words were so like some that Carlene had said to Grant on the fateful second date that she felt an affinity with Zoe. "Precisely."

Seconds ticked by as the two women sat in companionable silence.

Carlene took a deep breath and spoke again. "But I still want you to know that if I had realized you and Grant were a couple, I would never have shown up at his house like that."

Zoe met Carlene's gaze, her expression intent. "I know that, Carlene. I'll admit that I didn't at first, but later I realized that you weren't trying to hurt me, or Grant."

"Thank you. You can't know what a relief that is for me."

Zoe smiled. "I'm glad."

Carlene returned the smile, feeling warm. Amazing as it might seem, she believed she was making a new friend.

Win came out of the stable, dog tired, hungry and smelling like a horse. He'd spent the good part of last night and today with not one, but two foaling mares. Then Grant Strickland had come by and he'd had to have Joe give the other rancher the grand tour. But that wasn't what had him in a dreadful mood and had his insides clenching. It was something Grant had said.

They'd been standing in the stable outside the mare's stall and Grant had asked, "How is Carlene working out as your housekeeper?"

"Damn fine."

Grant nodded. "I can see that. To tell the truth, once I got to know her some, I had a hard time seeing her working as a cocktail waitress at the Dry Gulch."

Win couldn't see it himself, so he grunted in agreement.

Grant smiled, kind of with a wince. "Wish she'd gotten her job here a few months earlier though."

"Why's that?"

"I almost caked it up with Zoe over Carlene and I think I hurt her feelings too."

"What are you talking about?"

"I asked Carlene out, thinking I could use her to keep my distance from Zoe."

"She didn't tell me you two had dated."

"Don't know why she would. It wasn't exactly a big romance. One failed date and one failed seduction attempt." A look of guilt washed over Grant's features, as if the man regretted saying what he had.

Win felt his entire body tense. "You tried to seduce Carlene?"

Grant seemed to realize all at once that Win was more interested than an employer should be. "Uh...not exactly. Look, nothing came of it."

But Win saw something in the other man's eyes and he asked, "She tried to seduce you?" not believing it, but letting the words come out anyway.

"Forget what I said, Win. Carlene's a nice woman."

"Yes, she is. She's also mine." So much for being discreet, but he felt a very primitive, undeniable need to stake his claim.

Grant smiled, this time the look one of commiseration. "I get that. I'd build a fence around Zoe if she'd let me."

Win felt the same way and laughed, but something inside felt wrong. He couldn't get the thought out of his head that his innocent Carlene had tried to seduce the man in front of him. Another part of his brain denied the possibility vehemently. She would never have gone after Grant like that.

She wasn't the type and she'd guarded her innocence too damn strictly.

Carlene would have to be in love to give herself to a man and she'd given herself to Win. He had no doubts about her feelings for him.

Any more than he could doubt his feelings for her. Not any longer.

The sound of a vehicle on the drive brought his attention back to the present and he veered away from the back entrance to his house. Walking around the front, he saw Leah's car come into view.

She pulled up next to Carlene's stylish compact. Win couldn't help comparing his sister's family sedan to Carlene's bright red sporty coupé. There were a lot of other differences between the two women as well, but not where it counted. They both had integrity and they were both willing to sacrifice for the people they loved. He'd seen Leah do it time and again in her marriage and hadn't Carlene left her hometown to make life easier on her folks? They had something else in common too.

He loved them.

He'd reached that conclusion about three o'clock this morning as he soothed a hurting mare. He had not meant to love the feisty little brunette keeping house for him, but he didn't have a choice. After making love to her last night, he couldn't lie to himself about it either. They hadn't shared sex; they'd shared themselves. He wanted Carlene, but more importantly, he needed her. She brought sunshine into his life, as well as a passion he wanted to grow old with.

She wasn't anything like his mother. No more than Leah was. Carlene wouldn't grow bored with him and just move on. And unlike Rachel, Carlene wanted the same life that he did. A settled life, right here in Sunshine Springs.

Leah got out of her car. She looked exactly as Win had felt walking out of the stable a few minutes ago. Pain lanced through him at the knowledge that she'd gotten to that point because of her emotional turmoil, not something as simple as a birthing mare.

"How you holding up, baby-girl?" he asked, using the childhood nickname.

Her eyes filled with tears and she rushed into his arms. He closed them around her, wishing he could protect her with his love and strength, but knowing that this time all he could do was be there for her.

She didn't say anything. She just held on and cried for about five minutes. Finally, the storm of weeping passed. She pulled back from his arms. "I suppose you want an explanation?"

He shook his head. "No. I just want you to be happy."

She gave a small, watery smile. "Thank you. I don't think I'm ready to talk about it to anyone just yet."

He understood. Sometimes things needed to settle

before you could talk them out. "You ready to see the kids now?"

Her eyes lit up. "I'm dying to see them. I don't know what I was thinking, leaving them behind while I tried to figure out my future. They are my future and any decisions I make have to include their well-being."

Win's heart warmed at her words. He put his hand out and she placed hers in it. "Come on. I know two little kids that are gonna be real happy to see you. I want you to meet my new housekeeper, too. She's been helping me take care of the kids."

Leah stayed close as he led her into the house, her excitement at the prospect of seeing Shelly and Jared a palpable presence in the air around them. "What's her name? Maybe I know her."

"Carlene Daniels, but that may change soon."

He couldn't believe he was thinking about getting married again. After spending the night mulling over his newfound love and Carlene's request for him to define their relationship, he'd realized the only definition he'd been comfortable with had been one that included commitment. Permanent commitment.

He wondered how she'd react to the news. Probably totally differently than he expected. The woman was not exactly predictable.

Leah stopped dead still. "Who?"

"Carlene Daniels."

"The woman who used to be a bartender at the Dry Gulch?"

"Yes, but she's mine now."

Leah's eyes widened. "Yours?"

"My housekeeper." Other claims could wait until Carlene understood what they were.

"Oh, wow. And she's watching the kids?"

"Yeah. She did real good with them too."

"I…um…I wouldn't have expected that."

"You know Carlene?"

"Not personally, no. I just…I've heard of her. From Zoe."

"What did you hear?"

"Nothing important."

Leah tried to walk away, but Win wasn't letting her. He hugged her to him, refusing to go anywhere. "What do you know about Carlene?"

"Just she and Grant had a thing."

"One date and a failed seduction hardly makes a 'thing'," he said, borrowing Grant's words from earlier.

"So, you do know about it?" She laughed. "I guess Carlene is a lot less racy than I was led to believe if you've got her watching my children. I know how protective you are."

"Carlene is as far from racy as it's possible to get." The woman had been a virgin until last night.

"Her attempt at seduction must have been a one-time deal. She must have really been taken with Grant, I mean…" Leah's words trailed off as she realized she said too much. "I mean obviously it wasn't a big romance or anything."

But Win wasn't listening.

He was picturing Carlene with Grant and it was making him sick. "Let's go see the kids," he managed to force out.

Damn…after everything, was Carlene like his mom and Rachel after all?

He led Leah into the kitchen, then stopped and stared. Carlene sat in the middle of the floor, surrounded by dry pasta of every shape and size. Shelly and Jared perched beside her. It was Shelly wearing the apron this time.

She looked up and grinned. "Hi, Uncle Win. Me and Jared wanted to make sgetti."

"I's making noodles," chimed in Jared.

Carlene looked up at Win, her rueful smile and innocent eyes belying his sister's accusations. He saw knowledge of what they'd shared last night there too and it made him want to grab her and kiss her, ignoring his worries about what Grant had been to her. "I walked in here after putting a load of laundry in the washer and found Jared and Shelly practically buried beneath the pile of pasta. Defeated by their superior wit and speed, I decided to join them."

He felt himself smile in response to her teasing.

Leah laughed out loud. "Oh, you little hooligans!"

Before he could formally introduce Carlene and Leah, exuberant whoops sounded and the kids launched themselves off the floor and at their mother.

Leah dropped to her knees and gathered her children to her. She hugged them fiercely, whispering silly words of love and how much she had missed them.

Shelly pulled back from her mother's arms. "Mama."

Leah smiled. "Yes, dolly-girl?"

"I missed you."

"I missed you, too." Tears streaked down Leah's face, but she was all smiles as the kids dragged her to the courtyard to show her their toy sailboats in the fountain.

Carlene pulled out the broom and started sweeping up the pasta mess on the floor. "Your sister seems happy to be back with her children."

"She is, almost as happy as I'm going to be getting you all to myself again."

Carlene blushed. "Me too."

He pulled her to him for a quick, but hard kiss.

She smiled, looking a little dazed as she went back to sweeping. "I could get used to that."

"Me kissing you?"

"In the kitchen...just like a normal couple."

"We are a couple, honey."

"Is that right?"

"Yes."

"So, that's how you decided to define our relationship, the one that falls somewhere between a one-night stand and marriage."

Win grimaced, but Carlene didn't see it. Her attention was focused on the dry noodles she was trying to sweep together into a manageable pile. But he wasn't ready to discuss the life-altering decisions he'd made in the stable.

So, even though he knew it was not the right time to be talking about this, he asked baldly, "Did you try to seduce Grant Strickland?"

He didn't need Carlene to answer him. Her look said it all. She turned pale as milk and her lips trembled. She looked guilty as hell.

Indescribable pain lanced through Win. "Tell me you didn't."

"I can't."

He spun away and stormed out of the kitchen. He had to get away from her before he said or did something he'd regret until his dying day.

She'd loved another man enough to try to seduce him, but she'd made Win beg. The fact that she had given in and let him make love to her last night only seemed to make it worse, not better. He'd thought it was something better than he'd ever known, but if the evidence before him was any indication, she was more a master game player than Rachel had ever been.

Carlene had made him beg.

Carlene moved around her bedroom, packing her things. Leah was here now. There was no reason for the housekeeper to continue staying at Win's ranch. If he'd wanted her to stay, he would have said something. Apparently what they had between them—being a couple—didn't extend to the commitment of living together, or trust. As she folded the top she'd worn the night Win took her and the children out for ice cream she considered Win's reaction to her admission regarding Grant.

He'd just walked away. There had been no opportunity to explain, no chance to tell him she was sorry. Though why she should apologize to him for something that happened before they even met stymied her. It wasn't as if she expected him to apologize for marrying Rachel.

Win had taken Leah and her children into town for an early dinner and been avoiding Carlene ever since. That said it all, didn't it?

How had he known about Grant? Had the other man told Win? Or had Leah said something? After all, she and Zoe were friends. If that were the case, Carlene wondered who else Zoe had told. Was the tale of her botched attempt at seduction all over town? Carlene wished that Zoe had warned her, but she realized that was a foolish expectation.

Zoe was a really nice woman. If she'd told Leah, she wouldn't have expected the story to spread. Probably more than most people, Carlene understood how gossip worked. Even people who cared about you, like her parents, could do their share in spreading rumor and innuendo. Silence wasn't always golden and the truth could be taken out of context.

She pulled a pair of jeans from the closet and folded them before placing them neatly into the rapidly filling suitcase. She wasn't going to cry. There was still a chance for her with Win. It wasn't as if she'd demanded marriage from him. Surely, he wouldn't balk at being her lover because of the thing with Grant.

He just needed to cool down a little. She'd seen his possessiveness. He had a streak of it about a mile wide. He'd fired a stable hand he needed very badly simply because Lonny'd made a pass at her. He would get over his anger about Grant though. He had to. She didn't think her heart would survive if Win rejected her completely.

When she was finished packing, she carried her suitcase out to her car. Win was waiting, framed by the open front door, when she turned around to go back inside.

"Leaving?"

The covered entryway threw his face into shadow and she couldn't read his expression.

"Now that Leah's here, there's no reason for me to stay the night."

He didn't say anything and she couldn't stand the distance between them. Not the emotional or the mental one. She stepped forward until she could see his face, until she was close enough to reach out and touch him. His eyes were expressionless.

She put her hand out, touching his arm—feeling

the heat of his skin like a brand on her palm. "Win, we need to talk."

"Later, not now."

A lead weight settled where her heart had once been. "When?"

"I don't know. This just isn't working." He sounded so tired, as lost as she felt.

"What isn't working? Our affair? You're saying that you don't want me anymore because of what *didn't* happen with Grant Strickland?"

Win's eyes mirrored the pain she felt, but then his gaze turned hard. "I still want you." He raked her body with his eyes. "But that'll pass once you leave."

The words stung. Did he realize he could have slapped her and it wouldn't have hurt any more? He was making it sound as if she were just a body to him and she knew she was more. She had to be more. "Do you really think you can forget me so easily?"

For a brief moment the stoicism vanished and she saw her answer. Fear and pain mirrored in his eyes, but there was also anger. "I believe I have to try. Rachel did a number on me, but she had nothing on you."

"You don't mean that."

His stoicism cracked and he glared as if he hated her. "You tried to seduce another man, but you made me beg."

"It wasn't like that.

"I was lonely...depressed...I missed my real life. Grant came along and I don't know...I guess I thought we could have something. Something more than nights spent fending off advances from drunks and carding teenagers trying to buy beer on a dare."

"You couldn't expect him to marry you."

"No, we never even talked about it."

Win said a really ugly word.

"I didn't want to talk about marriage to Grant, Win. I didn't love him!"

"Are you saying you love me?" he asked, trying to sound like his old hard self, but she heard the emotion bleeding through. The need that matched her own.

Oh, please let it match her own.

"Yes, I love you, Win, and making love with you was a hugely scary step because of it. I knew I would lose myself."

"Did you?"

"Yes."

"You're leaving."

"I thought that was what you wanted."

"No."

"No?"

"Never."

"Never?" she asked, feeling light-headed.

"I don't ever want you to leave."

"That sounds an awful lot like marriage," she choked out.

"Doesn't it?"

"Win?"

"Come back inside, honey."

She nodded, her throat too clogged with tears to speak.

Carlene expected Win to come to her bed that night, but he didn't. She'd come back inside to find Leah waiting. The other woman had seemed keen to get to know Carlene. No doubt because she'd spent so much time with the other woman's children. Leah had thanked her profusely for potty-training Jared and then invited her to come to Portland to visit anytime she liked, the next day before she left town.

Win hadn't been cold to Carlene, but he hadn't acted like a man who wanted her to stay forever either and that oblique reference to marriage had her insides tied up in knots. He disappeared into town for a couple of hours after his sister left and then returned after the hands had eaten lunch.

He found her in the kitchen. He walked up behind her and kissed her neck.

She melted into him, the relief at his touch intense. "Hey big man. Did you get what you needed in town?"

"Yes."

She turned around to face him. "I want to talk. Is that all right?"

He nodded and then kissed her lips, softly, gently.

They went into the living room and he pulled her onto the sofa beside him.

She bit her lip and then made herself speak. "I didn't mean to make you beg."

"I thought you loved him more than me, but—"

"Oh, no," she said, talking over what he would have said next. "I didn't love him at all, but you…I think I've loved you since the beginning. And it scared me."

"You said you gave me your whole self when we made love."

"I did."

"That's going to make my next question a little redundant, but definitely necessary."

He pulled a small velvet box from his jeans pocket and laid it on her thigh. "Will you marry me, honey?"

She stared at the ring box and blinked back tears. When she made no move to touch it, Win flipped the lid up. Inside nestled the most beautiful diamond ring she'd ever seen. Its oval brilliance shone.

"Why is the question redundant?" she asked with a hitch in her voice she couldn't hide.

"You said you gave yourself to me, that means you're already mine. But I want the rest of the world to know it too."

"Do you love me?"

"More than anything in life. More than my fears. More than my certainty marriage is a trap for the unwary."

"I love you too."

"So the answer is?"

"Do you really have any doubt?"

"No." But his eyes said something else. "I wouldn't mind hearing an answer though."

She dropped to her knees in front of him and said. "Yes, Win. I want to marry you. Please, be my husband and my love for a lifetime. Please."

"You begging me, honey?"

"Love is worth pleading for."

"Yes, it is."

"What do you mean we aren't sleeping together again until after we're married?" Carlene demanded when Win kissed her outside her bedroom door and made to leave her there.

Alone.

Win watched her warily, but smiled. "I want to prove that I love you, that you're more than your body to me."

"You don't have to prove anything to me. We're past that."

"Yes, I do. You deserve it," he vowed. "You've spent your whole life being seen as a body and I need you to know you have always been and will always be more than just a sex partner for me."

"I know that, Win. You told me you love me…that you want to marry me, for goodness' sake."

She twined her arms around his neck and pressed against him. "Who appointed you the decision maker in this matter? I want to make love right now."

He grabbed her shoulders and held her away from

him in a cast-iron grip. "Honey, you are going to appreciate my restraint later. Trust me."

She laughed. "You are so darn arrogant."

He nodded, his expression pained. "I know."

What was she supposed to say to that? "Well, stop it!"

"I can't. Not this time. I need to prove to you that I love you enough to wait."

Of all the idiotic ideas...but also incredibly sweet and...she was not going to start crying. How had she ever gotten so lucky as to have this man return her love? "Win, that is ridiculous! I'm the one you're proving it to and I already believe you love me."

He smiled. "Good."

Finally. "So, we can make love now."

He shook his head, slow and easy. "No. This is important to me. Are you willing to wait for my sake?"

Darn him. He couldn't turn the tables like this. "Are you asking me to prove my love for you?"

"No. I know you love me, honey. You're willing to marry me knowing my worst flaws. I'm asking you to trust me. I'm asking you to let me do this right."

"Okay." What else could she say?

He let his hands fall away from her shoulders. "So, when are we getting married?"

She studied him for several seconds. "If we left now, we'd be in Reno by tomorrow morning."

He jerked as if shocked by a jolt of electricity. "What about the white dress and all the trimmings?"

"I've got a white dress. I don't care about the trimmings," she assured him.

"Your parents? Don't you care if they are there?"

She thought about that. "Nope. I'll send them an announcement. They'll be thrilled, of course. Married women are so much more respectable."

"I kind of thought we'd get married here in Sunshine Springs," Win replied.

She gripped the bottom of her top with both hands and peeled it off in one smooth movement.

Win gasped and his eyes turned dark blue. "What the hell are you doing?"

"Negotiating."

She put her hands behind her back, which pressed her breasts against the silk cups of her bra. She grasped the clasp on the back of her bra.

Beads of sweat formed on Win's forehead.

"Now, either you agree to Reno today or I unclasp this bra. I'm warning you. The next thing to go is my jeans. You're going to love my silk panties."

Win glared at her, but the unmistakable bulge in the front of his pants negated the intimidating effect of his stare. That and the fact that she knew he loved her.

"That's not negotiation, that's blackmail," he ground out.

She shrugged and Win's gaze zeroed in on her cleavage like an arrow to a target. "Call it whatever you like, but I'm one second away from taking this off."

Win swallowed and then he grinned. "How soon can you be packed?"

"Give me fifteen minutes." Then she bit her lip. "What about the stable?"

"The mares have foaled. One of the ranch hands can help Shorty and I can take a few days off, no problem."

Her smile was brighter than the noonday sun. "I'm so glad."

"Me, too, honey…me too."

CHAPTER TWELVE

Twelve hours later, Carlene unclasped the bra.

They'd flown to Reno and gotten married in the nicest wedding chapel Win could find and now he was getting his reward.

Carlene had her husband's full attention as she let the piece of white silk fall to the thick midnight-blue carpet of their honeymoon suite. Win's gaze was riveted to her beautiful breasts and the small scrap of silk that covered her feminine secrets.

"I told you that you'd love my panties," Carlene purred as she walked over to join him on the bed.

He'd already undressed and he waited for her on top of the white satin covering the huge round bed that dominated the room.

"They're every bit as sexy as the little white dress you wore to our wedding," he assured her.

As wedding dresses went, he had to admit that it had been unique. The white lace mini-dress that so obviously had been former work gear from the Dry Gulch lay in a pool at Carlene's feet. In fact, she had bought it to wear to work, but never got up the nerve to do so. He was glad. It had outlined her curves in a way that would have set more than one man's hormones roaring out of control. Win had been hard pressed to make it through the wedding vows. Literally.

Carlene covered the last couple of feet to the bed in a little rush. She landed against Win's chest, bearing him back on the bed. "This time, I'm going to lick you all over."

He grinned. "Sure you're up to it?"

She didn't answer. She was too busy licking a slow path down his throat to his collar-bone. She sucked lightly on the base of his neck and he groaned.

"Baby, that feels so good." He caressed her, brushing the sides of her breasts with his hands. "So do these."

She didn't answer, but kept moving down until she was making those sexy little circles around his nipples as she had the other night. Oh, man, he didn't know if he could take this. "If you aren't careful, honey, I'm going to lose it before I get anywhere near being inside you."

She laughed, the sound low and throaty. "I'm not worried, Win. I have tremendous confidence in your powers of rejuvenation."

Then she took his nipple into her mouth and sucked and he felt an electric jolt all the way to his penis. He bucked up off the bed and shouted something feral. He figured turnabout was fair play. He might not be able to reach her with his mouth, but he'd always had long arms. He started off by kneading the sides of her breasts until she was squirming against him, rubbing her hard little buds against his torso. He pushed against her until she lifted just enough for him to get his hands under her and play with the pretty pink raspberries.

She didn't stop torturing him with her mouth, though, and pretty soon she'd scooted down far enough that he was forced to reluctantly release the soft, velvety flesh of her breasts. She pressed wet, heated kisses down his stomach making him tense in anticipation of her going lower.

"Baby, maybe this isn't such a good idea. Let me love you."

She shook her head and her curly hair tickled against his lower abdomen. "You are loving me, darling, but it's my turn to pleasure you."

Who was he to disagree with the little woman when she got stubborn? Besides, it felt so damn good.

And then her hot little mouth was there, right on his engorged shaft and she was kissing the head with her tongue and lips. She made one long, slow pass from the tip of his shaft to the base with her tongue and then back up again before taking him back into her mouth and sucking. He wanted to explode, but not without taking her with him.

He grabbed her head and gently, but firmly, lifted her away from his erection. She murmured a protest, but he was past listening. He tossed her on her back and set about bringing her to the same brink he was trying so desperately not to go over yet. At the first touch of his mouth to her breasts, she cried out. By the time he'd suckled them both, she was writhing under him, her legs spread wide to make room for him.

He pressed his penis against the now slick opening of her body. "I'm not wearing a condom."

She stilled and met his gaze. "I don't want you to."

"Are you sure?"

"Yes. I want babies."

"Me too, honey. Me too." And then he was inside her and they were straining together toward ultimate fulfillment.

She cried out and convulsed around him, sending him over the edge, and he pumped his seed into her. "I love you," he shouted.

"I love you," she whispered in return.

Several hours and more than one bout of lovemaking later, she lay cradled in his arms. "Honey?"

She yawned. "Yes?"

"About your job."

She snuggled closer. "I like being your house-keeper, Win. It's fun cooking for the hands—though I'm not sure it's technically kosher for a wife to accept payment from her husband for that kind of thing."

He caressed her backside and wondered how soon

he could sustain another round of lovemaking. "I wasn't thinking about you being my housekeeper."

"You weren't?" She moved so that she lay on top of his chest, her chin resting on her hands.

"No. I don't think I mentioned it, but the principal of the high school is a friend of mine."

"She is?" Carlene sounded sleepy.

"Uh-huh. I gave her a call, she said that there's a position teaching English Lit for you, if you want it."

Carlene sat straight up, her nude body glowing in neon lights reflected through the window. "She said what? What about an interview? What about my résumé?"

Win chuckled. "Calm down, honey. The interview is set up for next week, but you're a shoe in."

"How can you be so sure? Did you tell her about what happened in Texas? I don't want to take a job and then have them hear about that debacle later. She'll think I lied to her, or didn't tell her the whole truth."

"I told her already, honey. She knew about it anyway. I guess you submitted your resume to the school district awhile back. She'd already run the checks. There weren't any openings then, so she didn't call."

Carlene nodded. "I never heard anything. There's an opening now?"

He reached out and touched the sweet bud on her breast. She shivered.

"Yes. It's only part-time, but I figured that would be okay with you."

"Any job teaching would be okay with me."

He reached for her and pulled her across his chest. "That's what I thought."

He kissed her, long and thoroughly. She was making sexy noises and moving against his body by the time he started trailing kisses down the side of her throat.

"Win?"

"Yeah, honey?"

"Thank you."

He stopped kissing her and took her head in his hands, forcing her to meet his gaze. "You could have done it yourself, but I like helping you."

She grinned, her eyes misty. "You're amazing."

Win's future stretched out before him, a golden road he would travel with Carlene, his wife. The wife he'd been sure he'd never have.

He flipped her over onto her back and set about making the other part of the dream he'd never even acknowledged come true. The dream of a family and a wife who loved him—who would love him for a lifetime.

THE ROYAL HOUSE OF NIROLI

*...International affairs, seduction
and passion guaranteed*

VOLUME FOUR

The Tycoon's Princess Bride
by Natasha Oakley

Isabella Fierezza has always wanted to make a
difference to the lives of the people of Niroli and she's
thrown herself into her career. She's about to close
a deal that will ensure the future prosperity of the
island. But there's just one problem...

Domenic Vincini: born on the neighbouring, *rival*
island of Mont Avellana, and he's the man who can
make or break the deal. But Domenic is a man with
his own demons, who takes an instant dislike to
the perfect Fierezza princess...

*Worse, Isabella can't be in the same room with him –
without wanting him! But if she gives in to temptation,
she forfeits her chance of being queen...and will tie
Niroli to its sworn enemy!*

Available 5th October 2007

M&B

THE ROYAL HOUSE OF NIROLI

...International affairs, seduction and passion guaranteed

VOLUME FIVE

Expecting His Royal Baby
by Susan Stephens

Nico Fierezza: as an internationally successful magnate, he's never needed to rely on his family's royal name. But now he's back – and the King has matched him with a suitable bride. Niroli is ready to welcome its new ruler!

Carrie Evans has been in love with Nico, her boss, for years. But, after one magical night of loving, he ruthlessly discarded her...and now she's discovered she's carrying his child!

Everything is in place for Nico's forthcoming nuptials. But there's an unexpected wedding guest: Carrie, who is willing to do anything to protect the future of her baby... The question is – does anything include marrying Nico?

Available 2nd November 2007

Mediterranean Men

Let them sweep you off your feet!

Gorgeous Greeks

The Greek Bridegroom by Helen Bianchin
The Greek Tycoon's Mistress by Julia James
Available 20th July 2007

Seductive Spaniards

At the Spaniard's Pleasure by Jacqueline Baird
The Spaniard's Woman by Diana Hamilton
Available 17th August 2007

Irresistible Italians

The Italian's Wife by Lynne Graham
The Italian's Passionate Proposal by Sarah Morgan
Available 21st September 2007